The Montanari Marriages
Wedding bells ring for the Montanari family...

Sister and brother Valentina and Rinieri Montanari
have never had time for love—in the Montanari
family, work comes before *everything* else.

Yet when romance blossoms unexpectedly,
will they both find themselves saying "I do"?

A hospital mix-up brings single mom Valentina
a whole new family in

The Billionaire's Baby Swap

Allesandra has always been overlooked in favor of
her more glamorous twin. Dare she hope billionaire
Rinieri is different? Find out in

The Billionaire Who Saw Her Beauty

Let Rebecca Winters enchant you with this
heartwarming and emotional duet!

Dear Reader,

If you've ever given birth and looked at your baby very carefully during the first few days, imagine your shock when you realize this baby couldn't be your child!

How would you feel when, two weeks later, you learn through DNA testing that it *isn't* your baby? This beautiful baby you adore belongs to another mother.

Where is *your* birth baby? Is it being loved by a mother who doesn't know she's got the wrong baby?

But you've already bonded with the baby you brought home from the hospital. Now you have to give it up to get your own back. How can you possibly let this baby go? Will you be able to love the baby who really belongs to you with the same intensity? How will the baby feel about you? How will the baby you've loved for the past two weeks feel about another mother taking over? Its *own* mother.

These are just some of the questions my heroine asks in this novel, *The Billionaire's Baby Swap*. On occasion in this world, two babies are accidentally switched at birth. It's a phenomenon that should never happen, but it does. You'll have to read this story to learn how all her questions are answered.

Enjoy!

Rebecca Winters

The Billionaire's Baby Swap

Rebecca Winters

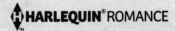

Recycling programs
for this product may
not exist in your area.

ISBN-13: 978-0-373-74380-3

The Billionaire's Baby Swap

First North American Publication 2016

Copyright © 2016 by Rebecca Winters

Printed in U.S.A.

Rebecca Winters lives in Salt Lake City, Utah. With canyons and high alpine meadows full of wildflowers, she never runs out of places to explore. They, plus her favorite vacation spots in Europe, often end up as backgrounds for her romance novels, because writing is her passion, along with her family and church. Rebecca loves to hear from readers. If you wish to email her, please visit her website at cleanromances.com.

Books by Rebecca Winters

Harlequin Romance

The Vineyards of Calanetti

His Princess of Convenience

Greek Billionaires

The Millionaire's True Worth
A Wedding for the Greek Tycoon

The Greek's Tiny Miracle
At the Chateau for Christmas
Taming the French Tycoon
The Renegade Billionaire

Visit the Author Profile page
at Harlequin.com for more titles.

To my wonderful father, who brought over 15,000 babies into the world.

At his funeral, our family was besieged with grateful mothers who loved their OB.
I miss him terribly.

CHAPTER ONE

AT FIVE TO three in the afternoon, Valentina Montanari finished her timed online engineering test and sent it into the testing site at the University of Naples Federico II. She could now forget her graduate studies for a semester and concentrate on the baby.

The strange backache that had come on during the test hadn't stopped. She got up from the table on the terrace, where she'd been working with her laptop and walked inside the villa to the kitchen for a drink. Maybe because of the way she'd been sitting, she'd developed a cramp.

"What's wrong, Valentina?"

She darted a glance at her brother's ever-watchful housekeeper, Bianca. "Oh, just a backache."

"When did it start?"

"While I was taking my test. Don't worry

about it." She poured herself a glass of freshly made lemonade. Bianca was a fifty-year-old treasure who cooked and cleaned for Valentina's older brother, Rinieri, who was still a bachelor. She watched her like a hawk.

"A backache this close to the due date could mean your baby is ready to come."

"I'm due July 6. That's four days from now. At my checkup last week, Dr. Pedrotti said the baby hadn't dropped yet and I might even go past my due date."

"All my babies started with a backache that never went away." The widowed mother of three no doubt knew what she was talking about. Right now Valentina wished her own mother were alive and here to talk to.

"The doctor said some backache was to be expected." She drank half a glass. "I'll walk around for a few minutes to work it off." But she'd only made it to the doorway of the kitchen when the pain reached around, gripping her like a pair of giant tongs.

"Caspita!" Valentina exclaimed. She braced herself against the door frame, surprised by the degree of pain.

Bianca nodded. "I *knew* it! I'm calling your doctor."

"I hate bothering him yet, Bianca."

The housekeeper ignored her and made the call. After a quick conversation, she hung up. "He says this could be the beginning of labor. First babies generally take a long time to be born, and your water hasn't broken yet. But he suggests you leave for the hospital. He'll check you out there. If it's a false alarm, no harm is done and you can come home. Rinieri said he'd be in Milan today, so I'll phone Carlo to drive you."

Before she could stop her, Bianca had made the call to Valentina's married brother, Carlo, who was two years younger than thirty-two-year-old Rini. After she got off the phone, she said, "Luckily he flew home early from Naples. He said he'd come for you right away."

"You shouldn't have called him. The pain is easing."

"Yes. But it will come back again and again. You get your things together."

"My bag is already packed," she called over her shoulder on her way to her bedroom to freshen up. Rini had already seen to that.

His nature to be in charge and have everything under control was the reason he'd been catapulted to CEO of the renowned Montanari Corporation at such a young age. Seven months ago her oldest brother had been the one to take care of her when she'd discovered she was pregnant. He'd talked her into moving out of the family villa in Naples and brought her to his villa a few kilometers from the vertical town of Positano.

Valentina adored both her brothers, but it was Rini who'd provided her with the emotional support she'd needed when she'd found out the father of her baby didn't want children or responsibility. Being abandoned by Matteo had damaged her confidence, and Rini had recognized that fact by being protective.

Once her relationship with Matteo was over, it was Rini who'd insisted she live with him instead of their father, who'd been grieving since the death of their mother in a car accident. He'd grown weak and needed a wheelchair more and more. He slept poorly. All he would need was a baby around the family villa in Naples.

Carlo had invited her to live with him, but she didn't want to intrude when he had a wife and child. She was blessed to have such wonderful brothers, but throughout her pregnancy she would have given anything if her mother had still been alive. They'd been so close. Now she was gone, and a grieving Valentina was going to have a baby without her mother's loving kindness and help.

A few minutes later she heard Carlo's voice talking to Bianca. Grabbing her purse and overnight bag, she walked to the foyer of the villa. He broke into a big smile and took the bag from her. "You're going to be a *mamma* in a little while. Let's get you to the hospital."

"I'm fine now."

"That's what Melita said before our little Angelica was born. Bianca was right to call me."

"Please don't tell Papà yet. He'll just worry."

"I agree."

She thanked the housekeeper and followed Carlo out to the courtyard, where his Mercedes was parked. As he opened the front passenger door, another pain took over. This one actually stung.

"Take some deep breaths until it passes, Valentina."

Carlo had been through this before with his wife. He had a calming effect on her. In a minute the pain subsided enough for her to get in the front seat. After some effort, he helped fasten the seat belt below her swollen belly. He patted her tummy. "Angelica's going to have a little cousin before long."

"I can't believe it's really coming."

"Don't be scared."

"I'm in too much pain to be scared."

He shut the door and walked around to the driver's side. Once behind the wheel, he started the car and they left the villa that was perched like an eagle's nest above the dizzying landscape of the Amalfi Coast.

The evening summer traffic impeded their progress to the main road leading to the Positano hospital. Valentina could see Bianca's wisdom in calling Carlo to come and get her. It would have taken Rini too long to get there.

Another pain, harder than the others, had taken over. She had a feeling this was really it. Her brother knew what was happening and let out a few epithets because someone was blocking the road.

"I should have brought you in the helicopter."

Normally unflappable, Carlo was showing a surprising amount of angst. If she weren't in so much pain, she'd smile because he seemed to be the one who was scared.

He honked the horn, but it did no good. At least a dozen cars were backed up with more cars lined up behind them. It took forever to reach the turnoff. The loud, blaring sound of a siren was getting closer. Another pain had started worse than the others. Valentina had always heard a woman comes close to death giving birth. If it was from the pain, she believed it.

"Carlo—my water just broke!"

"Hang in there. I'll have you at the hospital in a few minutes."

Suddenly there was a collision and the sound of twisting metal.

"Signor Laurito?"

What did his private secretary want now?

"*Si*? I'm just walking out the door to fly home to Ravello. Can't it wait until tomorrow?"

"This is an emergency. Signora Corleto is on line two."

His pulse raced. He knew his pregnant ex-wife could go into labor anytime now. He turned on the speaker to talk to his former mother-in-law. "Violeta? What's going on with Tatania?"

"Oh, Giovanni, the most terrible thing has happened! She started bleeding and we sent for an ambulance. On the way to the Positano hospital it was involved in an accident with two other cars. My precious *figlia*—"

She was crying so hard he could hardly make out her words.

"How bad is she?" The baby? His heart plunged to his feet. Had she lost it?

"The collision caused her to deliver the baby in the ambulance. Both are at the hospital on the third floor east wing. I don't care what she says. She *needs* you."

Giovanni needed answers, but she was too distraught to give him details. "I'll be right there."

He alerted his helicopter pilot, then raced out of the office and took the steps two at a time to reach the roof of the Laurito Corporation in downtown Naples. The flight to Positano took twenty minutes. After the short trip, his pilot set them down on one of the two helipads.

Giovanni waved him off and hurried inside the hospital. He reached the east wing and approached a doctor putting information into a computer at the nursing station. "*Scusi*—who can tell me the status of Signora Corleto and her baby?" When they'd divorced, she'd taken back her maiden name of Corleto.

The doctor looked up. "You are…?"

"Her ex-husband, Giovanni Laurito."

"*Ah.*"

"Signora Violeta Corleto, her mother, phoned and told me she'd been in an accident."

"That's correct. She's in with her daughter now. By some miracle she wasn't injured, but she had the baby in the ambulance before they could get her here. I'm glad you've come. I understand your ex-wife doesn't want to see the baby or keep him."

"That's right. It's been settled in court."

"Then that means you are the sole parent to your son."

"Si."

"Why don't you talk to the pediatrician in the nursery? I just came from there. Your baby is doing fine."

"And my ex-wife?"

"She lost some blood, but is recovering nicely."

"So she's out of danger?"

"Si."

Grazie a Dio.

"If her mother looks for me, tell her I'll be in the nursery." Violeta had never given up hope the two of them would be reconciled. That would be an impossibility.

"Go down the other end of the hall and through the doors. You can't miss it. Congratulations."

"Thank you."

Giovanni was still reeling with shock when he reached the nursery. The clerk alerted the pediatrician, who came out of his office to greet him.

"Signor Laurito, I'm Dr. Ferrante. Your ex-wife's doctor told me to expect you. You have a fine boy, who is doing well. Twenty-one inches long, seven pounds and five ounces."

"That's wonderful to hear. How soon can I see him?"

"Right now. Come in this other room and wash your hands. While you do that, I'll have the nurse wheel him in here, where you can hold him and inspect him all you want. Later she'll show you how to bathe and feed him."

Giovanni's heart started to pound hard. He'd played with the nieces and nephews from his two sisters' marriages, but he'd rarely held a tiny baby. To think this newborn was his own son!

When Tatania had first learned she was pregnant, she'd threatened to have it aborted. No doubt she'd wanted to punish Giovanni because of their failed marriage that she'd blamed on him. But her father, Salvatore, had threatened to disown her if she went through with it. His will had prevailed, *grazie a Dio*.

After removing his suit jacket and tie, Giovanni washed his hands and dried them with the automatic blower. The moment was surreal for him as the nurse pushed the cart through the door and smiled up at him.

"You have a beautiful *bambino*, Signor Laurito. Here. Put this cloth over your shoulder and you can hold him. He's asleep, but he'll soon wake up for his bottle."

He did as she said, but his eyes had fastened on the baby wrapped up in a crib blanket. His boy lay on his back. He had a beautiful face, almost angelic. Since Giovanni had black hair and Tatania was a brunette, the wisp of gold hair came as a surprise. His heart melted at the sight of him.

"Vitiello, *mi figlio*." That was an old family name he'd decided to give him after he learned they were having a boy. He'd call him Vito for short.

Without hesitation Giovanni picked him up and put him against his shoulder. The warmth of his tiny body seeped through him. "To think your first experience in life happened inside an ambulance. That's a story the whole family will talk about for the rest of your life." He kissed his cheek and neck.

Giovanni might not have given birth, but

his paternal instincts had taken over, and he was filled with a joy he hadn't known in years. His marriage to Tatania had never taken. Since the divorce he'd felt relief, but was pretty much devoid of any other feelings. She'd gone through the greater part of her pregnancy without Giovanni's help. To be united suddenly with his son thrilled him to the core of his being.

He couldn't comprehend that Tatania didn't want to coparent with him. According to the doctor, she hadn't asked to see the baby. If he knew Violeta, she would work on her daughter, but Giovanni didn't hold out hope. Every child needed a mother and father, but during their marriage, Tatania had shut down. It was as if every motherly instinct had been drained out of her. Psychiatric counseling hadn't helped.

Eager to examine his son, he put him on the changing board and unwrapped him down to his shirt and diaper. Being uncovered had wakened him. His eyes opened. Giovanni couldn't tell their color. Maybe a muddy slate blue.

He kissed him on either cheek. "I'm your *papà*. Welcome to my world." He checked his legs and feet that were wiggling. Those tiny hands had fingers that curled around his finger. Before long he would pull him up slightly to discover how strong he was. Laughter came out of Giovanni.

In a minute the pediatrician walked in the room and smiled. "It looks like father and son are doing well. The nurse will bring you a bottle and teach you how to feed him."

"Thank you, Doctor."

The rest of the night turned out to be pure delight as he fed and bathed Vito. By 11 o'clock Giovanni felt like an old hand, but he was exhausted. He arranged for his pilot to pick him up. He'd go home to sleep, then come back in the morning.

Once the baby was released, they'd fly home, where Stanzie and her husband, Paolo Bruno, were waiting for him. The attractive couple in their early forties had been managing the Bruno Advertising agency under their uncle Ernesto Bruno. Giovanni had become acquainted with the dynamic couple three years earlier through business. But months ago their uncle let them go because the business was failing.

Giovanni had stepped in to help them out and asked if they'd take care of his villa and garden for a temporary period. He believed in them and planned to set them up in their own advertising business a little later down the road that would benefit the three of them. Until that could be accomplished, he'd hired them to work for him, an arrangement that suited everyone. They'd been hoping to have children, but it hadn't happened yet and they could hardly wait for the arrival of the baby.

He'd spent the past month turning one of the guest rooms into a nursery with everything the baby would need. But nothing had prepared him for the sheer wonder of being a father. This tiny infant was his heart's blood. Already those protective feelings had taken root. He could tell his life had changed in ways he'd never dreamed of.

Two weeks had passed since the birth of the baby. Valentina looked down at her handsome son while he slept on his back. She was still trying to breast-feed, but the baby wasn't getting enough milk so she supplemented with formula.

She'd also struggled trying to decide on the right name for him before he was born. But once she'd laid eyes on him, she felt Riccardo suited him best. She'd called him Ric from that moment on.

"Did you name him after our grandfather?" Carlo questioned while they were gathered round in the nursery. Everyone was crazy about the baby, who luckily slept soundly.

"Yes, but let me ask you a question. I want your opinion on something. Because Matteo was blond, and I am, too, I didn't expect to have a baby with black hair. Dark hair does run in our family, but Ric's hair is a stark black. I don't know. Do you think Ric looks like our grandfather Riccardo?"

Carlo shook his head. "No. Not at all." Other than the dark hair, Valentina didn't see any similarities, either, but she'd had to ask. "This little guy has a distinct widow's peak."

"Papà noticed it immediately when he came to visit and thought it odd. Now I'm going to ask another question. Do you think he looks like me?"

Rini's eyes narrowed on her. "No."

"But he doesn't look anything like Matteo. He was blond and blue-eyed. My baby's eyes are dark already."

"Now that you mention it, Melita thought it strange he doesn't look like you."

At Carlo's comment a sick feeling grew in the pit of her stomach, and she turned away from the crib. "Let's not talk about it any-more."

"He could be a throwback to an ancestor, but none of it matters. Don't worry about it." Carlo kissed her cheek. "I've got to go home. Melita is waiting for me to help put Angelica to bed. Talk to you later." His footsteps faded down the hall.

Rini stayed in the nursery with her. "Valentina? Look at me." She was afraid to. "I know what has been going through your mind since you brought Ric home from the hospital. At first I didn't dwell on it, but tonight I have to admit I'm puzzled that I see no signs of you or our family in the baby. Before you turn yourself inside out, there's a simple way to learn the truth."

"I know," she whispered. "Get a DNA test done."

"Exactly. Then you'll know the baby is yours and you can stop driving yourself mad with worry."

Her breath froze in her lungs. "You wouldn't suggest my doing that if you didn't have doubts, too." Nothing got past her successful brother who was known for his genius in the business world. She held herself taut. "What if the baby isn't mine? I love little Ric with all my heart and soul. He's so gorgeous and so sweet."

They stared at each other for an overly long moment.

"Find out the truth first before you tear yourself apart."

Tears filled her eyes. "If he isn't my son, then it means that someone else went home from the hospital with *my* baby. Things like this just don't happen!" she cried out. The baby stirred before growing relaxed again.

"I agree switched babies are very rare, but it does happen. That's not to say that it happened to you, but to remove all doubt, call the doctor and have the DNA test done. I'll take you to the hospital in the morning and we'll get this thing settled."

Though she wanted to be more independent, she didn't know how she could do this alone and was grateful for Rini's loving support.

They hugged good-night and she went to her room, leaving the doors open so she could hear Ric when he woke up for his next bottle. Unable to sleep, she got on the internet and researched switched-baby stories. The latest one had come out of France. But the switch hadn't been discovered until twenty years later.

How horrible that must have been for both sets of parents. If Valentina's baby was given to the wrong mother, then she wanted her own baby back as soon as possible. But she wanted Ric, too. He was her very heart. How could she possibly give him up? They'd already bonded. Tears streamed down her cheeks.

Was there a mother out there who was worried that her baby didn't look like her, either, and wondered if some terrible mistake had been made? If so, then she'd already bonded with Valentina's birth baby. Valentina could hardly bear it.

She spent the rest of the night in agony. Instead of sleeping, she went in the nursery and sat in the rocker, holding Ric. The nursing just didn't give him enough milk. She fed him bottles to satisfy him at two different times during the night. Morning couldn't come soon enough. There wasn't any time to lose getting to the hospital to learn the truth!

Giovanni fed Vito his early-morning bottle before turning him over to Stanzie. He hadn't expected her to be a babysitter to Vito and had decided to hire a nanny. But when Stanzie heard that, she begged to do the honors.

In two weeks his boy was filling out and so much fun to play with, Giovanni had a hell of a time leaving the villa to put in a day's work at his office. He'd had visits from his parents and sisters since he'd brought the baby home. Violeta had begged to see him. He could hardly refuse her.

Giovanni realized she was a doting grandmother and could understand her pain over her daughter's refusal to see Vito. His son would be lucky to have the love of two grandmothers who already worshipped him.

After his flight to work, he met with Ernesto Bruno over a working lunch in his office conference room. The man's company did advertising for major companies, including the Montanari Corporation. For the last little while Giovanni had been working to buy Bruno's failing advertising business. He'd settled on a price that would be very lucrative for him. A win-win situation.

But by the end of the meeting, it became clear that Signor Bruno was still stalling. Maybe Giovanni had underestimated his loyalty to the Montanari family. It appeared the new CEO Rinieri Montanari, a shrewd entrepreneur, wanted to make Bruno Advertising a part of *his* company. Giovanni realized that in order to get to the root of the problem, he needed to go through Rinieri himself to settle this one way or the other.

He and Ernesto agreed to look at numbers and meet again in a week. After the other man left, Giovanni went back to his office to look over last month's accounts. He should have done it before, but Vito's arrival had consumed him.

Giovanni told his secretary to hold all calls. To his surprise she walked in on him, disturbing his concentration. "Signor Laurito? Forgive me, but there's a call for you on line two. It's Signor Conti, the administrator of the hospital in Positano. He said it was extremely urgent."

The administrator? Why?

He thanked his secretary and got on the phone. "This is Giovanni Laurito. You wished to speak to me?"

"I realize you're an important man, but something has come up I need to discuss with you. Could you come to the hospital this afternoon? Because of confidentiality, I can't talk about this over the phone."

Giovanni's brows knit together. Maybe this

was about Tatania. But if she'd changed her mind about seeing the baby, she'd go through her attorney surely, not to mention her mother. "I'll be there as soon as I can." He hung up and alerted his pilot. Before leaving his office, he called the villa to inquire about Vito.

"He's being a perfect boy and is taking his nap."

"That's good. Thank you, Stanzie. I'll be home for dinner. *Ciao*."

A half hour later he was invited in the administrator's office. "Thanks for getting here so quickly."

They shook hands and he sat down, but Giovanni was on edge. "Tell me what's wrong."

"I won't beat around the bush. Today we discovered that two babies from the hospital's nursery went home with the wrong mothers."

Giovanni felt his gut twist.

"This is the kind of mistake every parent dreads. One *I* dread. Someone in the nursery put the wrong band on the wrong babies. It is a terrible thing to have happened."

"How did you find out?" Giovanni's voice grated.

"One of the mothers came to the hospital with questions about her baby. He didn't look like her or the father. We had her DNA tested with her baby's DNA. The result proved that the baby couldn't be *her* baby."

Shock brought Giovanni to his feet. "Are you saying the baby I took home isn't mine and my ex-wife's?"

"No. We're having DNA tests on every baby boy that was in the nursery before this particular mother went home. Your baby is the last one on the list of eight we need to check. If you'll go to the lab, a technician will draw your blood and the necessary tests will be done along with your ex-wife's and son's blood to prove paternity. We need to do this process immediately so the babies can be returned to their rightful birth parents before any more time goes by."

"Let's do it now," he bit out, horrified that Vito might not belong to him after all. He thought of all the parents involved. Sixteen people were traumatized by the realization that their sons might have been one of the two to be switched. He swallowed hard. Was it Vito?

"I'll walk you to the lab."

They left the office together. "How long will this take?"

"In three days we'll know all the facts. The lab is rushing everything. Believe me when I tell you we'll move heaven and earth to make this right."

Giovanni grimaced. "Nothing could make it right."

"I know, and I can't tell you how sorry I am this has happened."

The administrator was taking this hard, as he should. Giovanni sensed that. But the thought of having to give Vito back to another set of parents was unbearable. If that happened, it meant his birth son was out there somewhere. Giovanni couldn't imagine having to give up the precious son he'd taken to his heart. But if his birth son was out there, naturally he couldn't wait to see him and hold him. This was a nightmare of impossible proportions.

After the blood was drawn, he flew back to Ravello. The second he entered the kitchen, Stanzie took one look at him and let out a cry. "What has happened to you? You're as white as a sheet!"

He looked her in the eye. If the impossible had happened, this was going to be hard on her and Paolo, too, not to mention his whole family and Violeta. Everyone was crazy about Vito. "There's a possibility that the wrong baby was sent home from the hospital with me."

"No—" She put her hands to her mouth. "In three days I'll know the truth."

Tears rushed down her cheeks...the same invisible tears he'd shed from the moment the administrator had explained his reason for the unexpected call. While he stood there in agony, she rushed out of the kitchen, no doubt running to tell Paolo the dreadful news.

Giovanni hurried through the villa to the nursery. Vito was awake. The minute he saw Giovanni, his arms and legs grew animated. His love for this child went so deep it could never be rooted out. He changed his diaper before carrying him to the terrace that overlooked the Mediterranean, where the scent of the roses was especially strong and sweet.

He kissed his cheeks. "I couldn't possibly give you up, Vito. We're going to forget that a mistake was made. You belong to me."

CHAPTER TWO

"SIGNORINA MONTANARI?"

Valentina recognized Signor Conti's voice. She gripped her cell phone tighter. *"Si?"*

"We have located your baby, even without the birth father's DNA. The DNA tests have proved that the baby you took home is a match for the blood tests of the couple whose baby was born on the same day as yours."

"Oh, no—" she cried out in pain. So it *was* true. The babies had been switched.

"I'm so sorry, *signorina.* You have no idea how terrible I feel about this, too. It should never have happened."

She wiped her eyes that kept dripping. "How was it possible?"

"I've learned that they were born within ten minutes of each other. After a full investigation is carried out, we'll learn the reason why the babies were tagged with the wrong mothers."

"Don't you know I'm dying inside?"

"Of course you are. That's why you need to be united with your son as soon as possible."

"And give up the one I already love?" she cried out in anger.

"Signorina—"

Weak from emotion, she sank down on one of the kitchen chairs. Valentina had been waiting for this day, yet dreading it. She felt guilty over her fear that she'd see the baby she'd given birth to and she wouldn't love it the way she loved Ric. It was a horrible thing to admit to herself, let alone her family.

Her birth baby had been loved and taken care of by another mother who had to be going through this same agony. The pain was so unbearable, Valentina could hardly breathe.

"Signorina?"

"I—I'm here." Shock that this day had come made her slow to respond. If she hadn't pursued this—if she hadn't said anything, then she wouldn't have to give up this little boy she adored. Her heart was torn into pieces.

"Since time is of the essence, if you can be at the hospital by noon with your baby, then the exchange can take place and your birth baby will be turned over to you. You need to be united with him as soon as possible."

She moaned. "I'm devastated, Signor Conti."

"I have no doubt of it. Do you have someone to help bring you to the hospital? You need to come to the outpatient entrance. When you sign in, you'll be told where to go."

"I—I don't know if I can do this." It took a minute to quiet her sobs. "Will I be able to talk to the mother who has been taking care of my baby?"

"It's not hospital policy."

"But that's cruel!"

"I'm sorry, but we have to treat this like a closed adoption process. Everything sealed. Your privacy has been insured. The other parents don't know your name, and you don't know theirs."

"I understand the legalities, but there are little things they should know about Ric."

"Of course. Why don't you write down your routine and any medicines and formula you're using, anything the other parent needs to know."

Sobs still shook her body.

"Signorina?"

"I'm here."

"I'll see you at noon. I realize this is very

traumatic for you. It would be for anyone. The hospital will have a counselor on hand to help you deal with your grief. We'll do everything we can for you."

Can you make it all go away?

"Again, I'm so sorry, *signorina.*"

She clicked off, unable to say another word. It was already eight in the morning. Only a few more hours before she had to give him up. Valentina hurried through the house to the nursery, where she found Rini holding Ric. He was dressed to go to work, but he loved the baby and sought him out at every opportunity.

"I just got the call. Ric isn't my baby. Your suspicions were right, too. I'm supposed to be at the hospital at noon to pick up my birth baby."

Rini grimaced. "I'll drive you."

"But you have work. I know you're having a problem with Signor Bruno and should be there to put out another fire."

"That can wait. Nothing's more important than helping you."

"I wish to heaven I'd never asked for a DNA test."

"You were acting on a mother's intuition that turned out to be inspired."

"But to pay this price—I don't think I can do it."

"Yes you can. Your birth baby is out there waiting for you. You're the strongest woman I know. Don't forget I'll be there for you."

She stared at the brother who'd been such a bulwark. "I know. You've always stood by me. I love you so much." Valentina had never done anything on her own and felt shame that she'd always been dependent on family. In showing such bad judgment with Matteo, she felt a failure, but her family had never made her feel like one. Right now she had to prove to herself how strong she really was.

"I love you, too, Valentina. More than you know. Can I help you pack up some things?"

"I'm not sure what to take, but I'll wrap him in the quilt I made."

Rini patted the baby's back. "The other mother will have everything Ric needs."

Tears filled her eyes. "You're right. I need to write down instructions for the parents since we won't be meeting. If you're willing to play with Ric, I'll get myself ready and make the list they'll need."

At eleven they left for the hospital in Rini's BMW. When they walked into the outpatient department and she'd checked in with her baby, she turned to her brother. "The woman at the desk said my family has to wait in the reception area."

He nodded. "I'll be right here."

"I'm glad no one in the family knows about this yet. I need time to deal with it first, then I'll tell Papà."

Rini gave her a hug before she turned away from him in pain. Signor Conti met her inside the double doors.

"Come down the hall to this room." Valentina clutched Ric to her heart while she followed him to a small room with chairs and a table. "Again, I'm devastated, *signorina*. This is a terrible situation, and I will do whatever I can to help."

She nodded in a daze. "What happens next?"

The second she'd asked the question, a nurse appeared at the door. Signor Conti looked at Valentina with anxious eyes. "If you'll give the baby to the nurse, then yours will be brought to you."

But Ric is mine.

Valentina's pain had reached its zenith. She broke down sobbing. "I don't know if I can do this, but I h-have to," she stammered. "If the other parents want to know, I named him Riccardo. Here's the list of information to give them."

Signor Conti took it from her. Valentina kissed Ric's cheeks, then gave him up to the nurse. She thought she'd die when the three of them left the room.

Is this really happening? Her body felt like ice.

In a minute the head of the hospital returned with the nurse, who carried a baby wrapped in a darling blue-and-white quilt. Valentina could hardly breathe as she walked over and put the infant in her arms. Signor Conti said, "I was told his name is Vitiello, but his nickname is Vito. I'll give you a few minutes to get acquainted, then I'll be back." He put a list made by the other woman on the table, and they both left the room.

Taking a deep breath she looked into the face of her birth son.

A cry escaped her lips.

Without doubt his facial bone structure was Valentina's. She saw shades of her mother, as well. Her beloved mother who was no longer here to turn to for love and advice. The baby had deep blue eyes. His pale blond hair— the way it grew—was hers and Matteo's. She carefully unwrapped him to check his toes.

He'd been dressed in a cute one-piece polo suit in navy and white. She could tell he'd been given perfect care and was thriving, but his little chin had started to wobble, tugging at her heartstrings. Valentina was a stranger to him, but she realized he belonged to her. All of a sudden he started to cry, wrenching her heart.

"Oh—my precious baby. I'm your real mommy, Vito. I know you're confused, but I already love you to pieces."

She put him over her shoulder. "You dear, dear little thing." She stood up and walked around, whispering endearments to comfort him. Right now she prayed that her darling Ric was feeling the same love from his birth mother. But the more she tried to quiet him down, the more he resisted, filling her with panic.

The head of the hospital came in Giovanni's room accompanied by a nurse. With the door open, he could hear a baby crying at the top of his lungs from another room. It was Vito! But Giovanni couldn't do anything about it because the nurse placed the baby in his arms. Then she left.

"His name is Riccardo," Signor Conti informed him. He put a list made by the other mother on the table. "I'll be back in a few minutes." The closed door shut off most of the sound.

Giovanni looked down at the baby. The second he saw his face and those dark eyes peering from the edges of an exquisite hand-stitched quilt in blue, yellow and white, he didn't need the proof of a DNA test to know it was his son. The telltale black hair and widow's peak proclaimed him a Laurito. His nose and mouth had the look of Tatania. He had long fingers, a trait of the Laurito men.

He could tell the mother had taken meticulous care of him. The one-piece navy body suit had four white sailboats. Giovanni was thrilled beyond belief at the sight of his son, but the baby wasn't happy to be with him and began to cry.

"Riccardo—*figlio mio*—I know you're frightened, but we'll become friends. You'll see." He raised him to his shoulder and ran his hand over his back. "I know you miss the mother who took care of you, but now you're home with me where you belong."

How shocking to feel this instant affection when he'd felt the same way about Vito. Seeing his own flesh and blood was like a miracle. He kissed his head and cheek while he walked around patting his little back to quiet him down. His son smelled wonderful.

But no amount of loving helped. If anything, the crying was getting worse. Vito had never cried this hard with him. Anyone hearing Riccardo would think something was terribly wrong.

Unable to stand it another minute, he scanned the list given him to find out if Riccardo had been nursed or drank formula. What he did see was the mention of formula. It was the same kind he'd given Vito.

Anxious to comfort him, he pulled out one of Vito's bottles and tried to get his son to drink it, but the baby was too upset and fought him.

Frantic because nothing was working, he opened the door to take him for a walk, anything to help him stop crying. Once out in the hallway, he heard Vito, who was crying hysterically. The sound came from another room around the corner and a long way down the hall. That was where Giovanni headed because two screaming babies needed comfort, rules or no rules.

As he reached the closed door ready to knock, it opened unexpectedly.

"Oh—" The mother cried to see Giovanni standing right there.

"*Mi scusi, signora.* I was just coming to find you."

"That's what *I* was about to do."

Despite the fact that both babies were crying at the top of their lungs, for a moment his gaze took in the angelic-looking woman. At first she seemed so familiar to Giovanni he couldn't understand. Then it struck him that it was because the son he'd taken home from the hospital and adored was a tiny replica of her, down to her blond hair. Good heavens, what a gorgeous woman!

But he couldn't go on staring at her when something needed to be done quickly to quiet the babies. "Let me take Vito."

"Yes. He doesn't want me," her voice trembled.

Giovanni felt her pain and grasped him in his other arm while handing a tearful Riccardo back to her. Without hesitation the exchange took place in the hallway. He didn't care if they weren't supposed to meet. Apparently she didn't care, either. It told him this terrible situation had nearly destroyed her, too. Already he felt a bond with her as she crushed Ric to her, yet never took her eyes off Vito.

After a few seconds their children quieted down and eventually blessed peace reigned. She looked up at him. Suddenly they both laughed in relief. In that instant he felt a tug on his emotions to discover this woman could find humor at such a precarious moment. She appealed to him in ways he couldn't begin to explain.

"Thank you for coming to our rescue." She sounded a little breathless as their eyes clung.

"I didn't know what else to do."

"I hear you. Where's your wife?"

"I'm divorced. She gave up her mother's rights."

Her incredible sapphire-blue eyes clouded. "I'm so sorry."

"It's past history. Is your husband here?"

She kissed his son—her son. "We never married. Our relationship ended a long time ago."

At this historic moment he had too many questions, but the hall wasn't the place for the kind of conversation they needed. "Why don't I grab the diaper bag out of the room I was in and join you in here so we can talk."

"Please hurry—"

That pleading in her eyes got to him. He understood the urgency and was gone and back in a flash. After closing the door, he dug inside the bag and handed her Vito's bottle.

She did the same with her bag. "Here's one for Ric."

He liked the shortened version. In a minute both babies had settled down and were drinking, totally happy to be in familiar arms.

Signor Conti poked his head in the room, shocked to see the four of them together. "So *this* is where you went, *signor*. It seems your babies found you."

"Our children don't understand hospital rules," Giovanni muttered. "But it wouldn't have mattered how this was handled, the babies need time to adjust."

He cleared his throat. "Under the circumstances, let me introduce you. Signorina Valentina Montanari, please meet Signor Giovanni Laurito."

Giovanni's body quickened. Such a prominent name in Italy's business world made him wonder if she was any relation to Rinieri Montanari, the new head at Montanari's. He was a hard man to do business with, forcing him to hold talks with Ernesto Bruno when he needed to meet with the CEO himself.

"I can see you two have a lot to talk about. This is a situation no one is prepared for. Since you've met, stay here as long as you need to. Remember we provide counseling if you feel that you need it."

They thanked him. Giovanni closed the door behind the administrator and sat down with Vito slumped against his shoulder.

She sat in the other chair and kissed Ric with all the love of a doting mother. He admired her for going through this whole experience without a husband to help her.

"Ric's hungry. I tried to nurse him, but I didn't have enough milk so he's been getting used to the formula."

"It looks like both babies have been on the same brand sent home by the hospital." He had dozens of questions but asked the first one on his mind. "How soon did you decide Ric wasn't your son?"

She darted him a glance. "From the first moment I saw him, I was surprised he didn't look at all like me. In the beginning I didn't say anything to my family, but after two weeks everyone agreed he didn't look like anyone on our side of the family. In the case of the baby's father, I saw no resemblance to him, either.

"My oldest brother knew I was worried and suggested I get a DNA test done so I could be absolutely certain one way or the other. My fear turned into a nightmare when the results came back, letting me know he wasn't my baby."

Giovanni nodded. "*Nightmare* is the right word, but I was the last person to be contacted by the hospital, so I haven't had as much time as you to be torn apart."

She smiled sadly. "No matter the length of wait, it has been a hideous experience loving our children, yet knowing we would have to give them up." Her gaze centered on him. "Now that I've met you, there's no question Ric is your son. His hairline and coloring match yours."

Giovanni was still trying to grasp the fact that their babies had been switched. "How much did he weigh?"

"The chart said eight pounds, four ounces. He was twenty-two inches long. He'll be tall like you. My baby's father was five foot ten. It explains why he's a little lighter and smaller."

His eyes lingered on her features. "Vito has so much of you in him, it's uncanny. I thought it odd that he was born with blond hair, but I never considered that he wasn't mine."

"My brother told me it was my mother's intuition."

Giovanni nodded. "If my wife hadn't refused to see him, she would probably have felt something wasn't right."

She expelled a deep sigh. "The mystery has now been solved."

"But not the agony," he finished the thought she hadn't spoken. "Our situation is so unique, there's no precedent to follow. I've read that out of four million babies born every year, twenty-eight thousand are switched temporarily, or permanently."

"I read the same article and was surprised it was that high," she murmured. "The doctor told me the car accident caused both myself and your ex-wife to deliver while we were in the ambulances taking us to the hospital. The mistake must have happened after we arrived at the ER."

His eyes found hers. "Were you injured?"

"No. I was already in labor. Everything happened so fast, I guess the impact sped up the process."

"The same thing happened to Tatania. She'd started bleeding, so her family called an ambulance for her. But she got the help she needed in time to recover with no aftermath of problems."

"Thank heaven."

"It's a miracle the accident didn't do more damage. I'm afraid my ex-wife's family will probably sue the hospital. Signor Conti hasn't said as much, but you know it's what he's fearing."

Valentina lifted the baby to her shoulder to burp him. "I can tell he's really sorry. He even offered counseling to help us. But as far as a lawsuit goes, I don't want to sue anyone. A ghastly mistake was made, but today it's been rectified. Surely whoever put the wrong bracelet on the boys had no idea what he or she had done. It happened." She kissed his little head. "No one's perfect."

"You're right." In a sue-happy world, Giovanni found her attitude not only amazing, but refreshing. In fact she appealed to him so much, he wanted to spend the rest of the day with her so they could really get to know each other.

"I'd better get going."

"Please don't leave yet." His mind raced ahead to prevent her from leaving. "I can understand why there's a rule that parents don't meet under a situation like this. The sooner we get our birth babies home, the sooner we can bond with them. But you and I *have* met. I'm not sorry."

After a slight pause she admitted, "Neither am I."

"Thank heaven you said that because I have to tell you I love Vito from the bottom of my soul. To forget him would be impossible. I want, need, to stay in touch with you."

Tears glistened in those fabulous blue eyes. "You've taken the words right out of my mouth. Ric is the most precious thing in my life. I held him all night, not wanting to let him go. Seeing the two of them together like this is tearing me apart. I know I have to give Ric up, but I can't bear it. If only there were a way to share them, but of course that's impossible."

He clasped Ric a little tighter. This was a place in Hell he didn't know existed. No way was he going to let her and his son just walk out of his life! He stared at her. "Maybe there is a way."

Her startled gaze met his. "What do you mean?"

"Since we both feel the same, I have a suggestion. After what happened today, it's clear we need time to spend together with both children so they get used to both of us. When they've learned to trust us and be happy with both of us, then we'll decide when we can safely make the separation, knowing it won't traumatize them."

"But how would that work?"

"You could stay at my villa with Vito for a few days. I'd get an extra crib. Then I could stay at your home for a few days with Ric. After a time we could separate and take one of them home with us and see how they handle being away from us overnight."

She averted her eyes. "According to everything I've read, that's exactly what we shouldn't do."

"Does it matter? We're talking about you and me and our babies."

Valentina bit her lip. "Even if it were possible, I'm living with my brother, so the idea of your staying at his house isn't possible." Giovanni Laurito had been a thorn in her brother's side. To consider getting involved with him when she knew how Rini felt made the whole situation precarious. Valentina couldn't believe the coincidence of both families having been brought together under such bizarre and astonishing circumstances.

"Where do you live?"

"Here in Positano."

"I live in Ravello. My home is open to you for as long as is needed. Why don't you fly home with me now so we can talk and make plans?"

She stirred restlessly. Much as she wanted to go with this man, Rini would never condone it. "People would think we were out of our minds."

"I don't particularly care. They would have to be in our shoes to understand how we feel. We're alone in this and we love both boys. Their welfare is all that matters. Don't you agree?"

"My brother would never permit it."

"Forget your brother for a minute."

He didn't know what he was asking.

"What is it *you* want? I caught you in the doorway wanting to find me, though you shouldn't have. I heard Vito crying and couldn't stay away from your door, either. Nothing about this situation has gone according to the book."

"I know," she whispered. "I—I need to think about it." Valentina was so tempted to go with him, it was killing her. The babies' needs aside, she felt an overpowering attraction to this man, who made her think and want things she'd thought were dead inside her.

"Then let's do this. We'll program our phone numbers into our cells. Since both babies are asleep, let's exchange them now. I'll take Ric home with me. You take Vito. We'll see how it goes tonight. In the morning we'll talk again. How does that sound?"

Valentina had to admit it sounded wonderful.

Though she didn't say anything, she reached in her purse with her free hand and pulled out her phone. He did the same. Once the programming was done she said, "My brother is waiting for me. I'll leave first before Vito wakes up and finds out he's with a stranger. Please keep the quilt I made for Ric. He's used to it."

"Did you make it?"

"Yes. My mother made beautiful quilts. I learned from her."

His eyes traveled over her face with an intensity that made her heart race. "You're remarkable, and can make something this beautiful and be a loving mother, too. I hope you know I'm in awe of you, and for going through this whole experience alone."

She felt his sincerity. His words boosted her confidence and thrilled her in a way he couldn't possibly understand. "I—I'd better get going." Her voice faltered.

"Be expecting my phone call in the morning."

Valentina knew herself very well. She was already hoping to hear from him. He could have no idea how much.

Her glance strayed to Ric. Her first impulse was to kiss him, but after a slight hesitation, she left the room, taking Giovanni's son with her in the quilt he'd bought him.

She walked out to the lounge of the outpatient department in a complete daze. The reality of Giovanni Laurito being Ric's father was stunning.

The *man* was stunning.

More than that, he was breathtakingly handsome, charming, reasonable and so loving to both babies it brought tears to her eyes. In a word, he was wonderful.

To think that all this time the famous CEO at Laurito's had been fathering Vito, *her* son. All this time Valentina had been mothering *his* son, Ric. The whole thing made reason stare.

She found her brother pacing the floor while he did business on his phone. As soon as he saw her, he put it away. How to tell him the true facts? She needed to think about it for a while first because she knew it would be a shock to him when he learned Giovanni Laurito was Ric's father.

"Sorry I was so long."

"Don't apologize for anything. Are you going to let me see my nephew?"

She nodded and turned the sleeping baby around so he could get a good look. "His name is Vito. He's so precious I can't believe it."

After a minute, her brother stared at her with a somber expression. "He's yours all right. Genes don't lie."

"No. They definitely don't."

"I know this is hard on you."

"You have no idea. Let's go. I want to get him home before he wakes up."

"I'll bring the car around the entrance."

"Thank you."

In a few minutes she got in the backseat with the diaper bag and settled Vito in the car seat. So far he hadn't stirred. She felt Rini's piercing gaze through the rearview mirror. If he knew what she and Signor Laurito had talked about, he'd quash the idea in a heartbeat.

No one had a greater right to an opinion than Rini. She owed him everything. But Vito's father had asked her a salient question. Is it what *you* want?

It didn't take long to reach the villa. She hurried inside with Vito and went straight to the nursery. Bianca followed her and grew misty-eyed. She'd loved Ric, too, but now that she could see Vito, she marveled over the likeness to Valentina and was smitten with him.

After putting him in the crib, she leaned against the bars and looked down at him. He truly was adorable, but she could never forget that this had been Ric's bed several hours before.

By now he was probably at his new home in Ravello. Signor Laurito's villa was a little over an hour away from Positano. Had Ric awakened and discovered she was gone? Her pain went so deep she broke down sobbing.

She felt Rini's arm close around her. He pulled her into him, where she buried her face against his shoulder. "I wish I could comfort you."

"You've done everything for me any human could ask for, but this is a problem not even King Solomon could make right. The truth is I want both babies." She lifted her head, aware that she'd soaked his shoulder. "They're both mine."

He kissed her forehead before releasing her. "I admire you more than you know for handling this with such grace and dignity."

For her brother to say that went a long way to make her feel better about herself as a capable person and mother. "I'm trying to, but I'm afraid Signor Conti is expecting the hospital to be sued." That was Signor Laurito's opinion.

"I suppose it's possible," he reasoned. "Look at the turmoil this has cost because someone made a serious mistake by not following the hospital rules. Everything about this has been handled wrong."

"I've been thinking about that." She sank down in the rocking chair, her eyes focused on her baby. "But everyone makes mistakes. Mine was worse for getting involved with Matteo when I knew better. He'd fed my ego and look what happened. But the person who put the wrong wristbands on the babies didn't do it willingly."

"That's one of the things I love most about you, Valentina. You have a generous heart. I can't think of another mother who wouldn't want justice after what has happened."

She flicked her gaze to him. "But what good would it do now? The damage has been done. Our mother would say the same thing. All I can do is love my birth baby and pray that God takes my pain away for losing Ric. It's so strange. I feel like I gave birth to both of them."

"I feel your sadness. What can I do to help?"

Valentina grasped his hand. "You're helping right now by listening to me. I couldn't have gotten through all this without your love and encouragement. But right now I'm exhausted. I think I'll lie down for a few minutes and ask Bianca to let me know when he wakes up for another bottle."

"I'll stay in here with him."

"I love you, Rini." She got up and kissed his cheek. Another glance at Vito and she went to her bedroom down the hall. Her body felt like it weighed a thousand pounds. She sank down on the bed and cried herself to sleep while visions of Ric and his striking father played in her mind.

When she was next aware of her surroundings, the baby was crying. She sat up. "I'm coming, Ric!" Valentina flew out of the bedroom, but when she reached the nursery, she discovered Rini holding Vito and she realized her mistake in thinking it was Ric. He was crying his little heart out.

She reached for him. "It's all right, Vito. I'm here, darling." She put him against her shoulder and walked around the room patting his back. To her surprise it was dark outside. She must have been asleep for hours. Her life had been turned around and upside down. Rini looked as tired and frustrated as she felt.

"How long has he been this upset?"

He flashed her a wry smile. "Almost from the moment he woke up and saw me looking at him. He needs you."

"I wish I were the person he wanted."

"Before long you'll be the mother he turns to."

Now was the time to tell Rini the truth of the matter. Valentina had made the mistake of getting involved with Matteo without the benefit of her family's knowledge until it was too late. If she planned to have any more contact with Signor Laurito, she didn't want to hide it from her brother, no matter if he didn't approve.

"Rini? There's something you should know. I found out Vito's mother gave him up at birth."

He frowned. "Is she mentally ill?"

"Maybe. She and his father are divorced, so it's the father I met at the hospital. His name is…Giovanni Laurito."

Her brother's eyes narrowed in reaction. "You must be joking."

She shook her head. "Signor Conti introduced us when he discovered we'd gotten together to quiet the babies. Nothing about this situation has been normal. But the point is, the children will have a hard time adjusting. Signor Laurito has made a suggestion that I've been considering to help the babies adjust."

A long quiet ensued. "What might that be?" he asked in a cool tone. When she told him, he took his time before responding. "Signor Laurito doesn't recognize boundaries."

Valentina swallowed hard. "Has he done something criminal?"

"No."

"Then what is it you have against him?"

"Ernesto did work for our company before Laurito discovered him. Now he wants to buy him out."

"Is that wrong?"

"No."

"Isn't that business? Invading someone else's boundaries?"

Her brother lifted his head. "Yes."

"But you don't have to like it."

"No."

"Thank you for being honest with me. In this particular case, I'm afraid I don't care about boundaries, either, not when it comes to our babies. Don't worry. I'm not making any decisions yet, but I wanted you to know everything." She hugged her brother. "Thank you for taking care of Vito while I slept."

"We managed to get acquainted," he said without referring to the other matter. "Right now he hasn't got any use for his uncle, but that will change. Bianca has your dinner ready whenever you want to eat."

"Thanks, but I'll wait until I can get Vito to quiet down. You go. You've lost a whole day to help me. I'm fine now."

"The family has called. I told them about the switch and said you'd get back to everyone in the morning."

"That's good. I'm not up to dealing with anything except my baby. Please plan to go to work tomorrow."

"If you're sure."

"I knew this would be hard, but I'll get through it. Bianca will help me."

"Okay." He kissed her cheek and left the nursery. She knew the revelation about Ric's father and his idea for getting the babies together had shocked Rini. But it was better he knew everything so Valentina wouldn't have to take on more guilt for remaining quiet.

She walked a whimpering Vito through the villa and out to the back terrace and the swimming pool beyond. "This is your home now, sweetheart." *But only for the time being.*

Then she would have to make arrangements to live on her own.

Valentina had intruded on her brother's life long enough. Though her father would do anything for her, she didn't want to put that burden on him. She needed to be on her own and take care of her baby and herself. Behaving like a grown-up was a start in the right direction.

"I'm a mother now, the head of my own family. We'll make it work somehow, Vito."

She kissed his wet cheeks. But no matter how much she tried to comfort him, he was unhappy. Maybe a bath would help. Unfortunately he didn't like it and cried throughout the whole ordeal. When he finally went to sleep with a bottle, it was two in the morning.

Valentina stole to the kitchen and warmed up the dinner Bianca had made for her. She needed food. If Vito woke up again and cried uncontrollably, she would need the energy to deal with him.

For the rest of the night she sat in the rocker. The baby woke up and cried several times. He drank his bottle but fussed through most of it. Around eight in the morning her cell rang just as she was holding Vito, who fought the bottle because he was crying too hard. *Please be Ric's father.*

CHAPTER THREE

VALENTINA CLICKED ON. *"PRONTO?"*

"Signorina Montanari?"

That deep male voice wound deep inside her body. Her heart thumped in reaction because she'd wanted to hear it again. In the background she could hear Ric crying.

"Yes." She was too breathless to say anything else.

"It sounds like you didn't get any more sleep than I did. Ric has been crying so hard, he's running a slight temperature."

"Oh, no—as you can tell, Vito's every bit as bad."

"We need to meet, if only to quiet the children for a few hours."

"I thought Vito would start to accept me, but it hasn't happened yet."

"I'm not Ric's *mamma*. What would you say if I came by for you in a few minutes and drove us to that park near the hospital? I've installed another car seat in the back. We can spread some blankets on the grass while we talk." Her pulse raced. "But if you don't want to do that, I'm going to the hospital and have Dr. Ferrante examine Ric in case something else is wrong."

"I'd rather meet you first to talk before we both lose our minds." She gave him directions to the villa and they hung up.

Valentina knew her brother would never condone it, but Vito's continual crying had made her frantic. As for Ric, she'd heard him wailing in the background. With Ravello more than an hour away, it meant Signor Laurito had been desperate for help. Something had to be done. So far nothing was working for either of them.

She put Vito in the crib and left him crying while she took a quick shower and opted to wear a skirt and blouse. After putting on lipstick and brushing her hair, she was ready. Before she left the room, she phoned her brother and left him a message that she was meeting with Signor Laurito today. Rini wouldn't like it, but at least she was being honest with him.

Once she'd packed the diaper bag, she lifted

Vito out of the crib and carried him into the kitchen in his carry-cot. "Bianca? Ric's birth father is coming for me. We're going to the park by the hospital in order to discuss our situation. I don't know when I'll be home. You can always phone if you need to."

"Does Rini know where you'll be in case he phones?"

"Yes. I told him Vito is so unhappy I've got to do something."

"That's true. The poor *bambino*."

"All he's done is cry. I've learned that Ric is just as miserable, so we're going to try and work something out. The exchange was too abrupt."

The older woman nodded. "The switch should have been caught before you ever left the hospital. Now that they've been home with you, they're used to you."

"I know. That's why we've got to come up with a plan."

"Vito's *mamma* is having the same problem?"

"Not Vito's *mamma*."

"What do you mean?"

"His *mamma* gave him up. His *papà* is raising him."

Bianca's hands clapped to her own cheeks. "The mother doesn't want him?"

"No. Poor Signor Laurito is frantic. During the call I could hear the baby crying in the background. He said Ric is running a temperature and needs to be checked by the doctor."

"Then you go on. When Riccardo sees you, he will calm down."

"Vito is suffering just as terribly." She went to the fridge and pulled out two bottles of formula. After putting them in the diaper bag, she said goodbye and hurried through the house to the front door.

When she emerged into the courtyard, she saw Signor Laurito waiting for her outside his dark gray Maserati sedan, wearing a black polo and stone-gray pants. This was the first time she'd looked at him in broad daylight and realized she hadn't been wrong about Ric's father. He was without question the most attractive man she'd ever seen in her life. He'd haunted her dreams last night. No wonder Ric was so handsome.

He reached for Vito and kissed him, then he put him in the back next to Ric and fastened him in.

"Where did you get another car seat?"

"When I brought Vito home from the hospital, I'd already bought a car seat for this car and one for Paolo and Stanzi's car—they're a couple who help me out around the house. This morning I installed it in mine, just in case you were amenable to going to the park with me."

After stowing the carry-cot in the trunk, he helped Valentina into the front seat. In less than a minute they were off to the park, with two infants crying at the top of their lungs.

Valentina happened to glance at him just as he looked at her. The situation was so crazy they both started laughing like they'd done at the hospital. He shared her sense of humor, something she loved. Between the noise all four of them were making, she couldn't seem to stop. The much-needed release from tension had affected him, too.

There wasn't much traffic. Before she knew it, they came to the park. He pulled the car to a stop near a copse of trees that provided shade. Valentina jumped out and plucked Ric from his car seat. "It's okay, darling." She pressed her cheek to his and could tell he was too warm. He snuggled against her.

Giovanni spread some blankets on the grass before claiming Vito from the back-seat. "Hey, Tiger. What are all the tears for?"

Slowly but surely quiet reigned. They laid the babies on the blanket and sat next to them. Two pairs of eyes, one blue and one black, stared at both of them.

Ric's father said, "Do you get the feeling they're sizing us up?"

Valentina wiped the tears from her eyes. "I can hear them saying, 'Why are you torturing us like this?'"

Their gazes met. "Before this goes any further, may I call you Valentina, or should I continue to call you Signorina Montanari?"

This tall, hard muscled male had a charisma she couldn't ignore. How was it that his marriage hadn't worked? His wife didn't want her own child? She couldn't comprehend it. Except that she couldn't comprehend Matteo not caring that she was going to have his baby.

"Please call me Valentina. And you?"

"I prefer Giovanni." He studied her features. "Does Vito's father *know* he's a father?"

"Yes." She played with Ric's fingers before scooping him up to hug him. "I was always a serious student and didn't date often. Much more important to me was to be like my brilliant engineering brothers and father. Because

I'm a woman, I wanted to prove myself in a household of male geniuses."

His head lifted. "So you *are* from the famous Montanari engineering family."

Something in his demeanor let her know the revelation had shocked him in the same way it had shocked Rini. "Yes. I'm close to getting my graduate degree in chemical engineering. Matteo, Vito's father, was one of my engineering professors."

"Ah. Tell me about him."

"I took two classes from Matteo before he asked me to come into his office to discuss the direction I wanted to go with my studies. I believed him to be gender blind and was flattered that my revered professor was showing so much interest in my future career. I accepted a lunch date so we could talk more without interruption.

"That led to other lunch dates. I admired his intellect and looked up to him so much, naive me couldn't see that all he wanted was to take me to bed, nothing more."

She saw Giovanni grimace.

"Reflecting back on last year, I'm positive he slept with other students from time to time. No wonder he has remained single. My attraction to him hadn't been physical. Since

I've come from a family of engineers, I was determined to get my graduate degree. Matteo was the one who'd seemed to take me seriously and listened to my ideas. He fed my ego by saying all the right things to make me feel important.

"When he told me how much he needed me and started kissing me, I succumbed even though it went against the morals of my upbringing. But after being with him one time, I couldn't do it again and told him I hadn't felt right about it. Not without marriage.

"He told me he never planned to marry. With that remark I knew I'd made a huge mistake. We parted company and I never planned to see him again. So no one could have been more shocked than I to learn I was pregnant even though he'd used protection. I notified him immediately. Not because I was hoping for a proposal, but to let him know he was going to be a father.

"Matteo told me a baby was the last thing he wanted and hoped I didn't expect anything from him. He thought I'd understood that from the beginning." She took a deep breath. "So unless he suddenly discovers he has a paternal instinct, I'll never hear from him again."

His jet-black eyes looked at her between black lashes. "What if he changes his mind and comes back wanting to start over and help you raise your son?"

"It's way too late for that. His utter selfishness killed any ounce of feeling I once had for him. If he were to show up demanding to see our son, I couldn't stop him from having visitation, but I can tell you right now he'll never come back. He's too in love with himself. It's an ugly story that happens far too often in society.

"One day I'll have to tell Vito the truth about his birth father. He'll think less of me of course, but hopefully the knowledge won't ruin his life."

This man was so easy to talk to it shocked her that she'd confided in him to this degree. It was time to change the subject. "What if your ex-wife decides *she* wants to be a part of Ric's life?"

By this time he'd picked up Vito and held him to his chest. "She won't. I'm the reason our marriage didn't work. I didn't love her the way she deserved to be loved, and I take full responsibility. When our divorce became final, she signed away all rights to the baby."

Her eyes widened. "Even though she was pregnant?"

"Yes. She conceived during a brief period of reconciliation, but we both knew our marriage wasn't going to make it. She moved back to her parents'."

"Where do they live?"

"Here in Positano. Two months after the divorce she called to tell me she was going to have a baby. Though she'd been on birth control, we discovered there'd been an antibiotic interference. The news couldn't have come at a worse moment, but I was overjoyed to think I was going to be a father."

She moaned. "How hard for both of you. So for seven months you haven't been together?"

He shook his head. "We've only been in touch through our attorneys. I was at my office in Naples when her mother called to tell me she'd gone to the hospital. Tatania doesn't want to hear my voice."

"How could that be?"

"She's angry with me for not being the man she thought she was marrying."

"I suppose it's human nature to want to change the things you don't like. I've never married, so I can't speak from experience. Did that make you angry?"

"Not angry, only frustrated with myself for getting married when I knew my deepest feelings weren't involved."

She shook her head. "Then why *did* you propose to her?"

He sucked in his breath. "That's a long story for another day. Right now I want to concentrate on our babies."

Valentina didn't dare press for more answers. "To think your ex-wife and I were both involved in that accident and gave birth on the spot is absolutely uncanny. Carlo told me the police gave the ambulance driver the citation for not taking more precautions no matter the emergency. But my brother is still upset and wishes he'd flown me to the hospital in the helicopter."

"It's water under the bridge now," he murmured. "We can thank providence there were no injuries."

Valentina nodded and reached in the diaper bag for a bottle to feed Ric. He made a lot of noise when he drank and wouldn't stop unless she pulled the bottle away to burp him. The second she put him to her shoulder, Vito let out the loudest burp she'd heard him make. His father burst in deep rich male laughter she felt coil inside her.

When she kissed his cheek before feeding him the rest of his formula, he felt cooler. There was nothing wrong with him that being with her again couldn't fix. He was so precious she didn't know how she could ever say goodbye to him. In her heart she knew Giovanni Laurito had those same feelings.

"Perhaps in time your ex-wife will come to you, desperate to see her son. If she did, I don't see you as the kind of man who would turn a deaf ear."

His brows met in a frown. "You don't even know me." He'd reached in his bag for a bottle and started to feed Vito.

"That's true, but I've seen you with your son. The way you love him tells me what kind of a person you are. You love him so much, you came to find him when you heard him crying. The hospital rules meant nothing to you. I'm sure you'd fight to the death for him. It's just something I know inside of me."

"Then we've met our match," he said in a low husky tone, "because you were willing to forget protocol, too. Otherwise you wouldn't have agreed to come to the park with me today when I know your brother would have forbidden it."

She blinked. "What does my brother have to do with my decision?"

"Possibly more than you think."

"What do you mean?"

"I've been putting two and two together. Your brother's name is Rinieri. Correct?"

"Yes." She averted her eyes. "But—"

"He and I have been undeclared business enemies for over a year. There was a time when I had a certain advertising agency in my sights that was in financial difficulty. I made an offer to buy out the owner because I like their work. But I found out he did work for your brother's company. I decided to make the man an offer to come to work for our company exclusively, and he said he was considering it.

"But your brother dangled a counteroffer in front of him, and now negotiations are at a standstill. Because of this, I do know your brother will never agree to the suggestion I proposed to you at the hospital about our spending time together with the boys."

Valentina felt a chill run down her spine. "When Signor Conti introduced us, I realized who you were. The Laurito logo is everywhere." She'd just put Ric down because he'd fallen asleep. "The one with the laurel wreath like the emperors wore."

His half smile quickened her pulse.

"I thought, 'You're *that* Laurito!'"

"I'm one of them. Our earliest ancestors came from Laurito near Salerno. In the early eighteen hundreds, one of my ancestors who was head of obstetrics in Naples came up with a stethoscope to hear the fetal heartbeat. Thus began the manufacture of medical instruments. It developed into major hospital equipment.

"Today that includes all types of machines to carry out research in medical and scientific laboratories. I've worked for some time on creating new advertising strategies for our company."

"How incredible."

"The advertising part is where your brother comes in to the conversation."

"I love and respect my brother, but he doesn't interfere with my making my own decisions."

"So if I asked you to come home with me today and stay as my guest for a few days while the four of us get acquainted, you wouldn't be worried how your brother will react? I wouldn't want to be the person to create friction between the two of you."

There was nothing she'd love more than to go with him. But at this moment she didn't know what to do, let alone what to say. While she sat there in a daze, he got to his feet. Vito had finished his bottle and slept against Giovanni's shoulder.

"At least this meeting has quieted the babies for now," he murmured. "I've found out there's nothing wrong with Ric except that he misses you. While they're both asleep, I'll run you back to your brother's villa. If Vito is inconsolable later and you decide you want to try the experiment we've talked about, then give me a call. If I don't hear from you, then I'll know you've decided that getting together isn't a good idea, after all. I'll respect whatever you decide."

He was such a good man, Valentina marveled. The thought of not seeing him again was unthinkable.

She eventually stood up and carried Ric to the car. Giovanni brought Vito along with the diaper bags and blankets. In a minute both babies were strapped in so they could leave the park.

He drove her home in silence and retrieved the carry-cot from the trunk.

She put Vito in it. Luckily he was still in a sound sleep. The knowledge that Ric was in the car was killing her, but what could she do?

"Our meeting did settle them down. Maybe it was all they needed and they won't be as upset from now on. Thank you for making it possible," she whispered and started toward the house. "I've enjoyed this morning."

"So have I. More than you know." His voice sounded husky.

The last thing she'd wanted to do was leave. Her attraction to Ric's father was so strong, it frightened her how much she could care for him after just two meetings with him. What was wrong with her?

Giovanni watched the lovely woman with the creamy blond hair and beautiful figure disappear behind the door. The double irony here was that he feared Ric wasn't the only male in the Laurito household who was going to miss her.

What were the odds of a baby switch that had thrown a Montanari and a Laurito together? She would have to be strong in her own right to go up against her brother, especially when he'd learned the name of Ric's birth father.

Giovanni could imagine their conversation. He'd tell her to forget another meeting. The baby would soon adapt. In truth, if Giovanni had a sister who'd been put in the same circumstance, he would tell her the same thing.

But Giovanni was the one embroiled in this cruel twist of fate. He loved both children and could hardly tear himself away from the villa when he knew Vito was inside. Since he'd told Valentina she would have to be the one to contact him, he had no choice but to drive back to Ravello without her.

He had hopes that if Ric woke up on the way home, he'd like the ride enough not to cry. The more he thought about it, the more he worried that he might have seen the last of his other son and the mother who'd given birth to him. He felt a sense of loss that was acute.

To his surprise Ric was awake by the time he reached his villa. When Giovanni removed him from the car, he didn't cry. *Grazie a Dio.*

"Oh—" When Stanzie saw them in the foyer she rushed over to kiss the baby's cheek. "His temperature is gone."

"We spent a few hours at the park. I think he liked it."

"Of course he did. He's much happier now."

"I'm going to change his diaper and put him in his baby swing on the terrace."

"Shall I prepare another bottle?"

"Thank you, but he probably won't want it for a while." Giovanni needed to call his assistant and tell him he wouldn't be in the office for a few days. Ric needed him even if his little son didn't want him yet. He wanted the mother who'd taken him home from the hospital. *So did Giovanni.*

Their lives had been turned upside down. He couldn't help but wonder what Valentina Montanari was going through right now. If Vito was being as difficult as Ric had been to this point, she was in for another sleepless night, too.

At 11 o'clock Rini entered the nursery while Valentina was giving Vito his last bottle. He'd been inconsolable all day. But for the moment he was so worn out from crying, he'd stopped fighting her and began drinking.

"How's he doing?" he whispered. "I had business in Genoa that made me late."

Vito heard his voice and his eyes opened before he stopped drinking. Then he started crying again. She put the bottle down and hugged him to her shoulder to quiet him.

"Sorry," Rini mouthed the word. "Why don't I hold him for a while so you can go to bed?"

"It won't work, Rini. He thought you were his daddy, whom he adores. He's still looking for him. If you'd seen them together today, you'd realize how difficult this is."

"Which is why you shouldn't have gotten together with him." Lines darkened her brother's face. "How can you expect Vito to forget?"

"I can't." She shifted Vito to her other shoulder in an effort to calm him down. "I need to talk to you about this, but it will take a while."

Rini pulled up a chair and sat down. "I'm listening."

"As you know, he's raising the baby himself because his ex-wife gave up her parental rights. She's never seen her birth son and doesn't want to."

Rini rubbed the back of his neck. "That's tragic."

"I agree. He called me this morning because Ric had been crying so much he was running a temperature. His plan was to take him back to the hospital to see if something else was wrong. We talked briefly and decided to meet because I haven't been able to comfort Vito, either. He came by the villa and drove us to the park near the hospital."

Her brother got up from the chair and stood there with his hands on his hips. All the while Vito kept whimpering. "He should never have called you."

"We exchanged phone numbers at the hospital in case of an emergency. It was a horrible moment. Vito was in one room, Ric in another. Both children cried hysterically after the exchange. I was frantic and opened the door to discover an equally frantic father standing there holding a red-faced Ric. We reached for our children and held them until they settled down."

Rini shook his head. "Whatever happened to rules?"

"I knew that was what you would say. As Signor Laurito stated, the children didn't recognize rules. Nothing about this situation has been normal. His ex-wife and I both gave birth before our ambulances reached the hospital where the switch took place. He loves Vito as much as I love Ric, and we find the situation impossible. I think his plan for us to spend a few days together will work."

"You think?" he blurted with uncustomary harshness. "You do realize who he is—"

"Yes. He's a brilliant CEO of his own company, just like you." In fact they were a lot alike. That was probably what was wrong. Within a few minutes she'd told him details about how Giovanni's company had gotten started. "I explained that I couldn't do this here at the villa, so he has invited me to stay at his villa with Vito for a few days, no more."

Her brother paced the floor for a moment, then stopped. "Despite the fact that I think the idea is a mistake, why did you rule out my villa?"

"Because this isn't my home. You've been wonderful to me, but I would never ask that of you. Especially when he told me the two of you are on opposite sides of a business transaction."

Rini looked surprised. "He told you *that*?"

"Yes. He's forthright and honest, exactly like you. I trust him. If Vito hasn't settled down by tomorrow, I'm considering doing it. I know I don't need your approval, but I want it more than anything."

A bleak expression crossed over his face.

"I want my baby to be happy. Vito didn't ask for this. Neither did Ric. His father is in agony just like I am. If we can give our children a better start by getting them to trust both of us, then we can separate them and it won't be such a horrible shock. What would be the harm in doing this?"

His head went back and he closed his eyes. "I don't have an answer for that. It sounds like your mind is made up. I love you, Valentina, and I'll support your decision, but I can't answer for the rest of the family."

"The rest of the family hasn't been here for me every day and night since you moved me here. I'm blessed to have a brother like you."

Vito was crying hard again. She got up from the rocking chair and walked around the room with him. Rini's gaze met hers.

"I'll leave so you can get him to sleep. I've an early-morning meeting at the office. Phone me when you know your plans."

Her eyes smarted. "I promise." She watched her brother's retreating back. There was so much he could have said, but he'd kept silent. Because he was wise and had so much integrity, that's why he was the head of Montanari.

A half hour passed and Vito finally fell asleep. Valentina went to her room and slept until she heard him crying around four. After that there was no comforting him. At eight in the morning she reached for her phone and called the one person who could end this nightmare.

"Valentina?" Giovanni answered on the second ring. "I trust your night was as bad as mine." His voice sounded an octave lower than usual, telling its own tale of another sleepless night.

"Vito's been awake since four."

"Ric finished off his three o'clock bottle and fussed off and on until ten minutes ago. He's sleeping, but before long he'll wake up looking for you. I don't want to live through another day like yesterday."

"I—I talked to Rini," she stammered. "He thinks getting the babies together is a mistake, but he said he'd support me in whatever decision I make. If you meant it, I'll take you up on your invitation to stay with you for a few days."

"You just said the words that saved my life. Ric and I will come for you. I should be there by 10 a.m."

"We'll be ready."

"*A presto*, Valentina."

After rushing to shower and wash her hair, she dressed in another blouse and skirt. Next she got busy packing for herself and some of the outfits she'd bought for Ric. Bianca was in the kitchen when Valentina went downstairs and poured herself a cup of coffee.

The first thing she needed to do was phone Rini. His voice mail was on. She left the message that she would be in Ravello and be staying for several nights. "Call me anytime, Rini. Love you," she said before hanging up, then drank most of the hot liquid.

"How can I help you?"

"I've got everything packed, Bianca. Thank you so much for all you do. You've been wonderful. All I can hope is that this experiment will help the four of us get acquainted. Hopefully the next time Signor Laurito brings me and Vito home, my baby won't be so unhappy."

She kissed Bianca's cheek and carried a suitcase and the diaper bag to the front door.

When she went back up to the nursery, Vito was crying again. She dressed him in another outfit and put him in the carry-cot with the blue-and-white quilt Giovanni had bought him with one of Mondrian's composition-type designs. He had wonderful taste.

"In just a minute you're going to be with your *papà*, Vito." She kissed his hot cheeks and carried him downstairs to the foyer.

Bianca had already opened the door. "The *signor* has arrived."

Yes. He certainly had. Today he'd come dressed in a white polo crewneck and jeans that molded to his powerful thighs. To her chagrin she realized she felt an excitement that didn't have anything to do with getting the children together. The man himself stood a class apart from other men. She'd scoffed all her life about the idea of love at first sight, but she hadn't met Giovanni...

For the first time in her life she'd been struck by a physical and emotional attraction so strong, she astounded herself. The fact that he was Ric's father only added to the attraction.

"*Buongiorno*, Valentina."

"*Ciao*! It has to be a better day than yesterday."

"Is there any doubt?"

No. There wasn't, not now that he was here.

She felt his jet-black eyes wander over her, bringing heat to her cheeks, before he picked up the carry-cot and gave Vito a kiss. She followed with the suitcase and diaper bag. Once he'd settled Vito in the car seat, he stowed everything else in the trunk.

Valentina would have opened the rear door

to give Ric a kiss, but caught herself in time. He wasn't crying right now. If he didn't see her, that would be better. She climbed in front and fastened the seat belt without a struggle.

"I see a smile on your face."

Valentina studied his rugged male profile. "Almost three weeks ago I struggled to get the seat belt around me on my way to the hospital."

Before he started the car he said, "No one would ever know you gave birth less than a month ago."

"Though you're a liar, I thank you."

His kind of deep male laughter excited her. He drove them out to the road leading to the coastal highway headed for Ravello. "Have you noticed there's no noise coming from the backseat?"

"Yes. I'm afraid to talk about it for fear I'll break the spell."

"Both my sisters have told me that when their children were babies, they often took them for a drive to get them to sleep."

Valentina nodded. "I heard the same thing from my sister-in-law. Since it's working right now, I couldn't be happier."

They followed the Amalfi Coast road beneath a golden Mediterranean sun. The car meandered five hundred meters above a turquoise sea. She could smell the fragrance from the lemon groves. Around each curb perched pastel-hued villas on the mountainside. No sight on earth could match it.

"You've got another smile on your face." He noticed everything.

"Though I was born and raised in Naples, I've always thought this is the most beautiful place on earth."

Giovanni nodded. "The locals call it 'the footpaths of the gods.' In my teens I rode my bike here with some friends from Naples. When we reached Ravello, I decided it was where I would live one day. Naples has a stifling effect on me."

"You're like Rinieri, who's also allergic to the crowded city. Early on he loved to rock climb and dive with his friends. They explored the Amalfi Coast and climbed to the top of the cliffs. He saw the turn-of-the-last-century villa he lives in now and decided he'd buy it one day. I never saw anyone work so hard to make that dream a reality." She looked away from him. "You must be a workhorse, too."

By now they'd reached the town of Amalfi. To Valentina it was a beguiling combination of mountains plunging to the sea with crags of picturesque villas and lush forests that took her breath.

"You've just described my ex-wife's reason for wanting a divorce." The unexpected revelation could explain one of the major reasons why their marriage had failed, but there had to be more to it than that. "Now that I have a son to raise, I've got to take another look at my life. I don't want him to grow up accusing me of never being there for him."

She bit her lip. "Was your father absent a lot?"

"Almost constantly. I see him more at work."

"I grew up in a family where the men were married to their work. Having observed my brothers, it's apparent to me that successful men have a hard time balancing their lives. Business has a way of consuming them."

"But it shouldn't," he bit out. "Since I'm going to be raising Ric alone, I'm going to have to change the way I do business."

"The fact that you want to be a more involved father is commendable."

He darted her a glance. "But you're not holding your breath."

"You've already been an amazing father to Vito or he would never have cried his heart out when he had to leave you. At the park his eyes followed you every second. Your bond with him is so strong, I'll admit I've been jealous."

"Then it shouldn't shock you that I've felt the same way about Ric's attachment to you. But if our plan works, our problems will go away."

Heaven willing. "Does your family know I'll be staying with you for a few days?"

"No. I've decided to proceed on a need-to-know basis. Of course, everyone knows about the switch."

"Are you worried that my staying with you will get back to your ex-wife?"

"Not at all, but for the time being it's no one else's business. My two older sisters have a bad habit of getting nosy."

Valentina chuckled. "My family is like that, too."

"Then we understand each other."

"Definitely."

"I take it your brother knows you're here with me."

"Yes. We talked last night."

CHAPTER FOUR

GIOVANNI DIDN'T COMMENT. Instead he made a left turn onto another road that climbed higher up the mountain. At the top sprawled the refined jewel town of Ravello with its dreamy gardens and magnificent views. Royals as well as composers like Wagner had stayed in the spectacular villas dotting the landscape. Valentina could understand why.

They kept climbing through a grove of green olive and lemon trees. He slowed down at the side of a stunning two-story white villa with burnt red tiles built in the Mediterranean style. Pale blue shutters adorned the windows. She'd thought there could be nothing more fabulous than her brother's ochre colored villa, but this place was spectacular.

Deep purple and red bougainvillea draped over the several terraces. A rock garden with palm trees formed a backdrop for the rectangular swimming pool. The profusion of flowers created poetry of such perfection, she wished she were an artist. Turning toward the sea, she gasped softly. "You live in heaven, Giovanni."

"That's what I thought when I first explored this spot years ago."

"Your darling Ric will grow up in a virtual wonderland."

Giovanni shut off the engine and levered himself from the car with a masculine grace he wasn't aware of. She slid out her side and they both opened the rear doors to get the children. Ric was still asleep, but Vito had awakened. His gaze fastened on Giovanni.

She smiled at him. "See how he searches for you?"

While he kissed her son, she plucked Ric from the car seat and followed his father across a patio into a fabulous sunroom. She gasped softly. It was circular in design with a tall ceiling and tall rounded windows filled with light that looked out on the gardens and sea below.

He kept moving through the breathtaking house to the curving staircase inlaid with stone tiles, enhancing the earth-toned colors of the surrounding landscape. Once they reached the second floor, he walked down a hall with a balustrade that overlooked a portion of the villa below.

"Your room is right here with its en suite bathroom." He opened the door and they entered a bedroom on the right. The moment she entered, she fell in love with the decor: oranges and yellows with cream walls and dark timbers overhead. An old armoire and an antique queen-size bed delighted her.

Over in another corner she spied a beautiful walnut crib all made up for the baby. She turned to him. "When did you get this?"

"After you phoned me this morning, I asked Paolo to run into town and get one that matches Ric's. He bought all the things to go with it. While I was gone, he put it together.

"As you know, he and his wife are here temporarily, looking after the house. They fell in love with Vito and now they love Ric."

"That's because he's made in your image," she broke in on him. Ric was still asleep. One day he'd be a heartbreaker like his arresting father.

"I'll bring up your things from the car and be right back."

She put Ric on the bed and changed his diaper, and then explored the room. The dresser had a hand-painted flowered design in the citrus tones. On the wall above the dresser was a large reproduction of the *Procession of the Magi* in marvelous colors, a famous fresco by Gozzoli. If Giovanni was the one who chose the art work, then it told her he was a man with many admirable facets, not the least of which were his parenting skills.

To think Matteo didn't even want to be told when the baby was born. For whatever deep-seated reason, Giovanni's ex-wife hadn't wanted to see her son. Both parents were missing out on the greatest joy of life and didn't know it.

Giovanni was still holding Vito when he arrived with her suitcase and purse. "Bring Ric with you and I'll show you the nursery. It adjoins my room."

She picked up the baby and followed him down the hall past the staircase. His room was clearly a man's bedroom. Through the open paneled doors she could see the charming nursery and an adult rocking chair.

The crib had a cute mobile of colorful fish. "How darling!"

"My mother helped decorate."

"It's wonderful."

He put Vito in the crib and changed him.

Out of the corner of her eye she saw a mini-fridge propped against the wall to hold the bottles. With Ric in the crook of her arm, she looked at the baby furniture and stuffed animals. She loved the little walnut rocking chair with Giovanni the Bear sitting inside it. In the bookcase several baby books were displayed, including her favorite, *Papa Piccolo, the Cat.*

"Oh, look, Ric. Elmer the Patchwork Elephant!" She drew it from the shelf and showed it to him. The toy seemed to distract him. "He's pink and yellow and blue. And he's soft." She nudged his cheek with it, then walked over to the mobile and wound up the little music box. It started to turn and played "*Giro Giro Tondo,*" a cute tune. Both babies watched the little fish go round and round. The music stimulated them and their bodies grew animated.

"You've learned to like that, haven't you, sweetheart." She kissed Ric's neck and cheek.

Giovanni's smile filled her universe with sunshine. He moved closer. In a low voice he said, "Do you know how great it is to be in here with no noise except the sound of the music box?"

Her heart pounded hard in her chest. With

the stress lines gone from his striking face, he was too gorgeous. She averted her eyes before he could catch her staring at him.

"Stanzie has fixed lunch and served it on the table in the sunroom. Let's take the children downstairs and put them in the playpen while we eat. There's a bathroom off the sunroom where you can freshen up."

Together the four of them left the nursery. "I love the layout of your home. How long have you lived here?" They started down the stairs.

"Three years. Tatania and I were married soon after."

She followed him past the living and dining rooms to the sunroom and put Vito in the playpen. "I'll be back in a minute." Valentina found the bathroom and freshened up. Once she'd washed her hands, she returned to see Giovanni leaning over the playpen. He was talking to their sons who appeared to be listening to him. The precious moment seized her by the throat and she fought tears.

This plan to help their babies get used to the change was a good plan. Everyone was happier. He must have sensed her standing there and turned around. "I finally have a chance to welcome you. The boys have told me they're glad to be here."

Giovanni... "I am, too." She was filled with so many new emotions bombarding her, she could hardly talk.

"Our plan is working, Valentina. You feel it, too. I know you do."

How could she possibly deny it?

When she would have found her voice, an elegantly dressed woman probably in her fifties with dark hair appeared outside the screen of the open double doors of the sunroom. "Giovanni? May I come in? I've brought a toy for the baby."

He looked over his shoulder. "Violeta— By all means, come in. I didn't know you were coming." In a few long strides he opened the screen door so she could enter.

"I tried to reach you, but your phone was on voice mail." She handed him a gift bag.

"I'm afraid I was too busy with the babies to check my messages. Violeta Corleto, I'd like to introduce you to Valentina Montanari. She's the mother whose baby was switched with mine and Tatania's."

The lovely older woman was obviously shocked to see Valentina there.

"How do you do, Signora Corleto?" Valentina crossed the expanse to shake her hand.

Ric's grandmother studied her with unsmiling eyes. Then she looked at Giovanni for an explanation. "I don't understand."

"The babies grew hysterical when we made the first exchange, so we decided to get together for a few days in order for them to get used to both of us."

Her dark brown eyes looked haunted. "I can't believe the hospital allowed you to meet each other."

"The hospital director handled things the best way he knew how. But the babies were so upset, Valentina and I sought each other out so we could comfort them."

"My husband is suing the hospital for what has happened."

Valentina took a steadying breath. "I heard your daughter had a hard time. Is she getting better?"

"Yes."

"I'm so glad. The odds of both of us being in a crash on the way to the hospital are astronomical. We just have to be thankful the babies are fine and thriving."

Giovanni picked up Ric and showed him

to his ex-mother-in-law. "Valentina named him Ric."

Tears filled the older woman's eyes. "Oh, Giovanni—he looks so much like you and Tatania." She touched his face, but Ric didn't like it and his chin wobbled. "Tatania needs to see him. Once she does, she won't be able to resist him."

Instead of a response Giovanni asked, "Do you want to stay to lunch? Hold him? Valentina and I were just about to sit down."

"No. I only came by to see him and bring a gift, but I've upset him. I'll call you later."

"Let me walk you out to your car."

"I'm so glad we met," Valentina called after her. She nodded and left. Valentina's heart sank to her feet to see the sorrow on the face of Tatania's mother. When Giovanni came back inside, she said, "I feel so sorry for her. There've been too many shocks."

"You were very sweet to her, Valentina. Seeing her daughter in the baby made it all the more difficult to accept the fact that Tatania doesn't want anything to do with Ric."

"It's so sad."

"Time will heal the wounds." He put Ric in the playpen. "Shall we eat? Stanzie is a great cook."

The rest of the day and evening turned out to be pure pleasure as they ate and played with the babies.

"How did Stanzie and Paolo come to work for you?"

"It's an interesting story. Their last name is Bruno."

"You're talking about the same Bruno as my brother."

He nodded. "They managed an advertising agency for his uncle Ernesto," he explained. "Over several years I often ate lunch with them while we discussed ideas to expand the advertising for Laurito's. They're some of my favorite people.

"But Ernesto wasn't a visionary man and the business was failing. Paolo had some brilliant ideas. Unfortunately his uncle wouldn't listen and it reached a point where he let them go."

"He did that to his own family?"

"Afraid so. I asked them to work for me at the villa until I get them set up in another advertising business I plan to run."

"So that's why you were in competition with Rini?"

"Yes. I wanted to buy out Ernesto so Paolo and Stanzie could go back to managing the business the way they wanted. But your brother saw a great business opportunity, and it's still up in the air which way Ernesto will go. Please don't say anything to your brother, who would have his own ideas about the people he wants to hire. It's a private matter."

"I wouldn't interfere, but I admire you very much for trying to help."

"Paolo and his wife are amazing people with real talent. While they're living with me, I've arranged for someone to rent their house in Naples."

"And I have to tell you that Paolo and Stanzie are darling with the babies."

"It's a shame they couldn't have children of their own."

"Maybe there's still hope. I know people who had babies in their forties."

"I've told them the same thing."

By the time they decided to take the babies upstairs and bathe them, Valentina felt like they were a family.

The nursery had its own en suite bathroom. They took turns giving the babies their baths. Giovanni put Ric in the water first. "You like this, don't you?" He washed his dark hair with the baby shampoo. Valentina handed him a big fluffy towel after he lifted him out of the water.

"It's your turn, Vito." She filled the sink with fresh water and then gave him his bath. He didn't like his head shampooed, but he didn't actually cry. "See. This feels good. You and your brother are being very brave."

Valentina realized her mistake before Giovanni handed her a matching towel. His eyes were smiling at her slip. "That just came out." She hugged him to her and carried him into the nursery.

Giovanni diapered Ric and put him in a white babygro for bed. Then he flicked her a glance. "If you want to know the truth, when we were in that hospital room, I kept thinking they were like our nonidentical twins."

Our twins. Her breath caught at the thought.

"Well, tonight should be a lot of fun for them. Their first slumber party." She heard him chuckle before she put a little blue babygro on Vito. After sitting in the rocking chair, she fed him his last bottle. Giovanni brought a chair in from his bedroom and did the same with Ric.

As long as they were both in the room with the babies, there were no tears. Only the sounds of the boys drinking rather noisily disturbed the peace and quiet. After being burped, Vito fell asleep first. She left him on her shoulder. He was her little angel. At this point she loved both babies so much she could hardly stand it.

Ric finally passed out with his bottle. Giovanni put him in his crib, then signaled Valentina to follow him into the bedroom. He patted the bed. She lay down on one side and put Vito in the middle. Giovanni stretched out on the other side. They turned toward the sleeping baby and smiled.

This was like playing house, except this wasn't a dollhouse and none of them were dolls.

Giovanni was a full-grown, breathtaking male. Her bones melted with the way his eyes devoured her.

"Do you know this is the first time I've felt this content in years? How about you?"

She nodded. "Once I started undergraduate school, I put pressure on myself to succeed. The stress increased when I got into graduate school. Then I lost my mother, and her death devastated the whole family for a long time."

"I can only imagine," he commiserated.

"I could go to her about anything, Giovanni.

She knew I suffered from an inferiority complex and told me I had to believe in myself no matter what." Her eyes smarted. "I'm wondering now if she hadn't died, would I have gotten involved with Matteo?"

Giovanni reached across to give her arm a squeeze. "But if you hadn't, we wouldn't be lying here with our little boy who has brought so much joy into our lives. It's why I can't be sorry about my marriage to Tatania even though it ended. Ric is a living miracle."

"They both are," Valentina whispered.

"Thank you for accepting my invitation." His voice throbbed.

"I'm thrilled to be here, but it's getting late so I'll say good-night and take Vito with me." She was loving this way too much. Using every bit of willpower, she rolled off the bed before gathering Vito in her arms.

Giovanni followed her out of his room to her bedroom down the hall. She felt his eyes on her as she put Vito in the crib. "Please remember this house is yours while you're here."

"I will. If you need help, I'll hear the crying and come."

"That works both ways, Valentina. *Buonanotte.*"

After this wonderful evening, she didn't want to say good-night, but to have stayed on his bed any longer would increase her desire to stay with him all night. She wanted to lie in his arms and be kissed senseless by him. How crazy was that!

"Good night."

Giovanni groaned to have to walk away from her. He wanted to stay and make slow, passionate love to her. In all his adult life he'd never known desire like this. But it was too soon to show her how he felt. She needed time to get to know and trust him.

Though the babies were the reason they were together at all, it was the woman herself he'd also been drawn to from the first moment she'd opened the door at the hospital. He loved the way she loved the babies with a fullness of heart.

Valentina had been fearless in defying hospital policy in order to make them happy. When it came down to the wire, she'd forgotten herself in the need to protect her children. Those actions told him reams about her character.

He got ready for bed and slept with one ear open. At ten after three he heard Ric start crying. Throwing on his robe, he hurried into the nursery to change his diaper and feed him. As he reached for a bottle from the fridge and put it in the microwave to warm it up, Valentina came in the room with a fussy Vito. She was a vision in a nightgown and pale yellow robe.

Her eyes searched his. "I'm glad you're up. Vito must have awakened at the same time as Ric. Vito's still looking for you. I heard Ric fussing and thought we'd join you."

Giovanni grinned. If she only knew, he'd willed her to come. *"Benvenuta al Caffetteria Laurito, signorina."*

Laughter bubbled out of her as she sat down to feed Vito. He plucked Ric from the crib and sat next to her, thinking this was the way marriage should be. Two parents who'd lost sleep, but were crazy about each other and their babies.

The children could hear both their voices. Long after the babies had dozed off again, he and Valentina were deep in conversation about his life. "Did you always want to work for the family business?"

"Not in the beginning. I went to Sapienza University in Rome, thinking I might pursue medicine."

"What changed?"

"My father's constant urging that I join the company."

"Because he needed his son behind him."

"My mother and sisters said as much."

Valentina eyed him thoughtfully. "Are you sorry you didn't become a doctor?"

"No. I've found there's a strong bent for business in my blood. I derive a certain excitement from winning over a new account."

"You're probably sick of my asking you all these questions."

"No, Valentina. You couldn't be more wrong about that. It's so easy to talk to you, I feel like I've known you all my life."

"I feel the same way, but I'd better take Vito back to bed before I wear out my welcome."

Lines darkened his striking features. "Don't you know you could never do that?"

She looked away quickly and hurried out of the room with Vito, leaving him bereft. He went back to bed and slept till seven when Ric needed another bottle.

After showering and dressing, he took the baby downstairs and walked out on the patio, where he found his guest with Vito. She saw him coming.

"Good morning. I couldn't resist coming out here this morning. All this lavender wisteria thrives in such huge clumps, it's fantastic. And the smell is so heavenly, Giovanni. I've always heard that Ravello is the garden town of the Amalfi Coast, but in my opinion it could be the Garden of Eden. You should charge admission."

He chuckled. "The last thing I want is a stream of people invading my inner sanctum."

"I know that." She smiled. "I was only teasing you."

"The garden and sunroom are the reasons I bought this place. I spend most of my time in the sunroom, where I can wander outside on a whim. Every flower has its season to bloom. I'm constantly delighted myself."

"I think you have an artist's soul."

"What makes you say that?"

"The painting in my bedroom by Gozzoli."

"At Christmas our mother used to read to us from a storybook about the Magi with that same painting on the cover. I was always fascinated by it. Last year I happened to see the reproduction in a store, taking me back to my childhood. I bought it on the spot and put it in the guest room."

"I love it. I love the way the room is decorated, the colors. The nursery is adorable with its charming touches. I love your villa, the setting, everything! Forgive me for going on and on about it, but I just can't help it."

"Your opinion means a lot to me. Shall I bring your breakfast out here?"

Color filled her cheeks. "You've done too much for me already by allowing me to mother your son a little longer." The tremor in her voice tugged on his heartstrings. She swept past him and entered the house. It took every ounce of self-control not to reach out and pull her into his arms.

She put Vito in his carry-cot and sat down at the table. "Another feast," she exclaimed when they'd finished eating.

"Wait till you eat the lunch Stanzie has prepared for us."

Valentina's gentle laughter warmed his insides. "You're still hungry?"

"I will be because I'm taking you and the babies out for a picnic."

"Where?"

"It's a surprise. On the way we'll stop in town for another carry-cot stroller so we can push the babies around."

They went upstairs to get the children

ready. While he dressed Ric in a yellow sun-suit, he flicked her a glance. "Do you know I'm having the time of my life?"

She'd put Vito in shorts and a blue-and-white-striped shirt. "Can you believe these are the same unhappy little boys of a few days ago? Vito isn't fighting me this morning. I think you were inspired to suggest we work together to help them adjust." She flicked him another glance. "You do know that your un-orthodox methods explain why you're run-ning your family's company. You get results!"

"Let's hope it continues."

"So far so good. Vito's going to help me get my purse, then we'll meet you downstairs."

Before long they left the villa, loaded with a hamper full of food and bottles. Giovanni drove them along a road that led to town. After they'd made their purchase, they got back in the car and wound their way to the famous site of the Villa Rufolo.

"I've heard of this place."

"An Englishman built a strange concoction of structures, cultural elements and mixed styles, but it's the villa's garden you'll fall in love with. We'll enter through the tower, then walk around first. Later we'll come back to eat near the temple over there."

* * *

Valentina couldn't wait to get started. Once they fastened the babies' carry-cots in their strollers, they were ready to go. The whole property filled with statues, fountains and an ancient cloister enchanted her. Giovanni was better than any tour guide and incredibly patient as she asked question after question.

Eventually they reached a terraced garden that offered fantastic views of the Church of the Annunziata and the brilliant blue water of the Mediterranean below. "According to Gore Vidal, this is the most beautiful spot on earth."

"It's certainly one of them."

They walked back to the car. Giovanni got out the hamper and carried it to a grassy spot while she pushed both strollers behind him. He spread out a blanket, and they let the boys lie down on their backs while she and Giovanni ate.

Her gaze swerved to him. "Tell me something. You don't mind showing me around when you've probably done this before with your ex-wife?" Valentina didn't want to be jealous of her; still, she couldn't help that she would have loved to know him a long time ago.

"If she came here, it wasn't with me. She

preferred my apartment in Naples when I had to stay there for business. She often told me how isolated she felt here in Ravello."

"Some people need a big city."

His dark eyes pierced hers. "What about you?"

"I'm a lot like my brothers. We love being on top of the mountains looking down to the sea."

She changed the babies' diapers, then got out two more bottles. Together she and Giovanni fed them while they soaked in the heavenly atmosphere. When her cell rang, it startled her. She drew the phone out of her skirt pocket. It had to be one of her family. Her dad's caller ID showed up. She clicked on. "Papà?"

"How's my daughter?"

"I'm great. How are you?"

"Missing you."

"I've missed you, too." More than he could know.

"When am I going to see my grandson?"

"Very soon."

"Carlo and Rinieri told me about the switch. They say he looks exactly like you. You always were our most beautiful baby."

Tears filled her eyes. "Papà... I promise I'll come to Naples."

"Rinieri said he'd bring you and the baby tomorrow."

Uh-oh. If Rini said that, then he was holding Valentina to her assurance that she'd only spend two days away to help the children adjust to the change.

"If all goes well, I'll see you then. I love you, Papà."

Until she hung up she didn't realize Giovanni had gotten to his feet. His nearness and male potency assaulted her senses. "Is everything all right?"

She took a big breath. *No*. The thought of leaving him in the morning had disturbed her more than she wanted to admit. "Yes," she lied. "It was my father. Rini told him he was flying me to Naples tomorrow so he could meet his grandson."

His jaw hardened perceptibly. "So you've already talked to your brother?"

"No. But when I told him our plan about the babies, I said I would only be away a couple of days. Apparently he took me at my word and let my father know I'd be bringing Vito."

He stood there with his powerful legs

slightly apart. The light breeze disheveled his black hair. His coloring and olive skin made him too gorgeous. "I see. Naturally you don't want to disappoint your father. In that case I'll drive you back to Positano first thing in the morning. But until then, let's enjoy the time we have."

She lifted her eyes to him. "I *am* enjoying it." Way too much. "So are the babies."

He walked over to the hamper and pulled out a soda. "Do you want one?"

"Just water. Thank you."

"Do you think our boys are going to handle another separation so soon?" He handed her the bottle and sat down by her.

"Probably not, but in all honesty, will there ever be a good time?"

Giovanni took a long swallow. "I've been asking myself the same question and the answer comes up no."

They needed to make the decision to separate for good and get on with their individual lives, but the thought upset her too much. "Still, we don't have to worry about it today. You've gone to a lot of trouble to make it possible for us to enjoy this fabulous time together."

"Give me a minute to carry the hamper

back to the car, then I'll help you put the babies back in the strollers so we can leave."

By nine that evening, the day out for the picnic had come to an end. They'd returned to the villa, where the babies had been bathed, fed and put to bed. After thanking Stanzie for the delicious packed lunch and the dinner she'd served upon their return, Valentina said good-night to Giovanni.

When she reached her room, she texted her brother.

Rini—I'll be home tomorrow around ten. Spoke to Papà. I've told him to expect me and Vito tomorrow. Lov u.

She'd kept the message short. Rini would vet her on the flight to Naples.

Valentina looked around the bedroom and decided to get packed. Afterward she showered and washed her hair. A day at the Villa Rufolo meant she'd picked up some sun. It felt good.

Once she'd blow-dried her hair, she put on a nightgown and got ready for bed. A knock on the door prompted her to slip on her robe. She tied the sash and walked over to open it.

Giovanni's dark gaze drifted over her, sending her heart palpitating.

"I didn't realize you were ready for bed."

"We'll both be up in the night. I thought I'd better catch as much sleep as I can."

Lines darkened his handsome features. "When do you want to leave in the morning?"

I never want to leave.

"I texted my brother and told him I'd be back around ten."

"Then we ought to get away by eight thirty." She nodded. "Valentina?"

"Yes?"

"I had a wonderful time with you. It was an extraordinary day." He stood too close.

"I agree. I've been hoarding the memories."

"I don't want it to end." His voice grated.

She put her hands in her robe pockets in order to hide her nervousness. "I don't, either, but now that the babies aren't so upset, we know we have to make that final break."

"Says who?" he challenged.

Valentina averted her eyes. "Says everyone. Conventional wisdom."

"I've been doing things all my life to please other people. For once I want to do something *I* want to do."

She let out a sigh. "When I was thirteen,

one of my teachers was lecturing our class about the rules. She said you can do whatever you want in here as long as it doesn't hurt you or anyone else. It made a lot of sense."

"I had a teacher who said the same thing, but we're talking about our children. They had a different start than most children. Why don't we capitalize on what has happened?"

If her heart pounded any harder, he'd be able to hear it. She lifted her head. "What are you suggesting?"

"That we go on seeing each other."

"It won't work, Giovanni. If we don't stop this now, Vito will always be looking for you. That's not fair to him or Ric."

"Even if it will make them happy?"

"They'll be happy. Give them a few days away from us and they won't remember us anymore."

His eyes flashed. "You want to make a bet?"

"Giovanni—" She shook her head.

"Let's give it two more days and then see how they react apart from us. I don't want you to leave." He unexpectedly cupped her face in his hands and kissed her lips.

His mouth on hers sent a bolt of electricity through her body. With a soft gasp she moved away from him. "We mustn't do this.

It won't work. We have to say a final good-bye tomorrow."

"You could rearrange the time with your father."

"I could, but I won't and you know why. Now I'm going to say good-night."

She closed the door and leaned against it, terrified she'd give in to anything he had to say. Valentina touched her lips. He'd awakened a new longing in her. If she did what he was asking, then she'd be putting her own selfish need ahead of her son's needs. What Giovanni was asking just wasn't possible.

Rini had warned her it wasn't a good idea to see Giovanni again. She'd thought she could handle it. She'd wanted to handle it for the babies' sake, but she hadn't counted on caring for Giovanni to this extent. After Matteo, she thought she'd learned her lesson and couldn't imagine ever getting close to another man again. The love for her baby would be all that mattered to her.

After another minute, Valentina opened the door again so she could listen for Ric. Then she turned off the light and slipped out of her robe. Once in bed, she buried her face in the pillow. That way she could smother her tears. Tomorrow she would have to be strong.

Tonight she couldn't help but give in to the emotions roiling inside of her.

Giovanni's kiss was all she could think about. Ever since the hospital, he'd infiltrated her thoughts. Her Vito had gotten his start with the kind of exceptional man she hadn't known existed. It was all turned around. Now there were two babies she loved with every atom of her body. Worse, she'd fallen deeply in love with Giovanni. There was no other explanation for the reason he'd taken up lodgings in her heart.

CHAPTER FIVE

A WEEK LATER when Giovanni saw the name on the caller ID, he picked up. "Stanzie?"

"Forgive me for disturbing you at work. I know I've done it every day this week, but I don't think Riccardo likes me or Paolo. If you want to hire a nanny, maybe you should." He could hear in her voice she was close to tears.

There was only one woman Ric wanted when Giovanni wasn't there. This business couldn't be allowed to go on. "Of course he likes you, but he's still not used to the change. I'll be home early and we'll talk."

After he got off the phone, he alerted his pilot, then told his assistant to reschedule any appointments because he was leaving for the day. A half hour later he'd hired a limo with a car seat for an infant to drive him from the helipad in Positano to the Montanari villa. He told the chauffeur to wait.

Giovanni used the wrought-iron knocker to bring someone to the door. If it was Rinieri himself who answered, so be it, though he imagined he was still at work. With no results the first time, he knocked again.

When the door opened, he heard a gasp. "Giovanni—" Valentina held Vito in her arms. She sounded like she was out of breath and had hurried to the door.

"I had to see you, but if I'd phoned, I feared you wouldn't pick up."

The sound of his voice must have brought Vito's head around. The second he saw Giovanni he made jerky arm movements and started to cry. Though she held him fast, he kept looking at Giovanni instead of hiding against her and cried harder.

"He wants you," she murmured. "He's been looking for you all week. Go ahead and hold him."

Giovanni didn't need an invitation. He drew him into his arms and cuddled him against his chest and shoulder. "It's only been a week, but you've grown!" Vito cried a little longer, then rested peacefully against him. "I've missed you, too, Tiger."

He glimpsed tears in Valentina's eyes. She looked tired but beautiful in a sleeveless top and shorts. "Your bonding with him was so strong. Rini doesn't fill the bill, wonderful as he is."

Rejoicing that she'd admitted it, he tried to give Vito back to her, but he clung to him. "I'll tell you why I'm here. Stanzie called me at work a little less than an hour ago and said I needed to hire a nanny because Ric doesn't like her or Paolo. I told her I was coming home. After we hung up I flew straight here, knowing what needs to be done. Ric misses you terribly. Nothing has been the same since you left the villa."

She wiped her eyes. "Maybe you could bring Ric here and I'll take care of both babies for a few days. Then I'll take Vito there and you can watch both of them for a few days. It would mean rearranging your work schedule."

He shook his head. "That won't work and you know it. I'm as exhausted as you are trying to comfort Ric, so I've come to ask you to move in with me. For how long I have no idea. Unfortunately the babies had just enough time to get attached to both of us, so instead of trying to fight the obvious, let's get together for the sake of their happiness and our sanity."

Valentina eyed Vito. "It's true that if I tried to take him from you right now, he'd have a meltdown."

"Ric was having one when Stanzie called."

An anxious expression broke out on her face. "If we get together now, it can't be for too long. Otherwise it would cause too much damage to the children and I wouldn't be able to handle it. But there's another risk. You know how people talk. I was never married. People would say I was a loose woman using you for what I could get out of you."

"People could say I got rid of Tatania because I'm a womanizer who wanted you and that's why we're divorced. None of it's true."

"You admit it could create a scandal both our families would have to live with."

"My parents learned a long time ago I make my own decisions."

"But your mother-in-law—"

"No matter what, she wants to be a grandmother to Ric. I say to hell with what anyone else thinks! Our babies were switched at birth and nothing has been normal about it."

After a pause, she said, "I know what Carlo would say. Get over it and lead your own lives."

"And Rini?"

She looked away. "He hasn't said anything, but he's aware of how Vito has behaved. H-he knows how much I mourn the loss of Ric," she said, her voice faltering.

"If you asked your father, what do you think he'd say?"

"To follow my heart. That has always been his advice."

"Did you ask his advice about Matteo?"

"No. I already knew he wouldn't approve of my getting involved with a professor so much older."

That was news to Giovanni. "How much older?"

"Twenty years."

That explained a lot about the engineering professor having a midlife crisis with a student as utterly delectable as Valentina. No doubt it fed his ego to seduce the daughter of one of the celebrated Montanari engineering family.

Giovanni nuzzled Vito's neck and kissed him. Her fragrance went where the baby went. "He gave you a beautiful son."

She swallowed hard. "He did."

"So what *does* your heart say now?"

There was an interminable silence while he waited for her answer. When she looked at him, he saw more tears. "You already know the answer or I would have closed the door on you before Vito got the chance to realize who it was."

Relief swept through him in waves. "I have a limo waiting. Go ahead and do what you have to do to get ready. I want time to play with Vito. We'll walk around out here."

"I'll have to leave a message for Rini and a note for Bianca. She went to the market."

"Take your time. You don't have to bring everything yet. There'll be other days to come back for more things. We're in no hurry."

He wandered around the courtyard, admiring the explosion of flowers and Rinieri's exquisite taste in buying this two-story villa. Its design reflected a bygone era of elegance and refinement. Like Giovanni, Rinieri had his own helipad at the rear of the estate, but he wouldn't have been so presumptuous as to use it.

When he saw Valentina come out the front door, he strapped Vito in the car seat, then helped her put her things inside. She disappeared once more for the carry-cot. While he'd waited for her, she'd changed into white pants and a top of navy-and-white stripes that outlined her womanly figure. The sight of her ignited all his senses.

Once everything and everyone were installed, he instructed the driver to take them back to the Positano helipad. He let Vito cling to his finger. She studied the two of them. "Look how excited he is to be with you."

"If you think he's happy, wait till Ric discovers you on the premises." Their eyes met. Her tears were gone.

"I pray we're doing the right thing, Giovanni. Down the road—"

"Don't think about that," he interrupted her. "Let's enjoy the here and now. The future will take care of itself." He had plans for them, but after her experience with Matteo, he didn't want to make a wrong move.

Within minutes they lifted off for the short flight to his villa in Ravello. Though he'd bought it and made it his own, he'd never felt like he'd really come home until the helicopter set them down.

Paolo and Stanzie were out in the garden that bordered the swimming pool, tending Ric. They waved when they saw him climb out. But he hadn't come alone. When they caught sight of Valentina, Stanzie cried with excitement and hurried toward her with Ric.

"Welcome, Valentina!"

"It's good to be back, Stanzie."

Ric heard her voice. Just like Vito, he started wiggling to get to her. This time Giovanni's eyes filled to see the way he cried and burrowed into her neck. His son knew exactly where he wanted to be. He took after Giovanni in that department. This moment was one he'd treasure all his life.

Valentina rocked Ric in her arms. Over his little head with its black hair she looked at Giovanni. Without being able to resist he said, "Remember that bet I made you a week ago?"

She nodded. "They *do* remember us and it's been a lot longer than two days."

"If you hadn't been such a terrific mother, Ric wouldn't have suffered so much. I say we all go for a swim."

"Won't the water be too cold for them?"

"We'll pull them around on the rafts."

Her blue eyes lit up. "That sounds fun. I'll hurry inside and change. Come on, Ric. You can help me."

Stanzie wasn't ready to give up Vito.

Giovanni followed Valentina into the house with her suitcase. After he set it inside her room, he headed for his own room to change. He threw off his suit and tie, so anxious to get outside he didn't care about anything else. After pulling on a pair of brown-and-white trunks, he grabbed some towels and hurried out to the back patio.

A couple of children's toy plastic rafts rested against the wall. He tossed them in the water.

"Come on, Vito. We're going for our first pool ride."

He smiled at Stanzie, who gave him up. Hugging him to his chest, he carried him into the pool. After settling him on his back in the middle of one of the rafts, Giovanni started moving it around at the shallow end.

"Don't be scared. Your mommy's going to be out here in a minute with your brother." That was the second time the word had slipped out. While he moved him around he caught sight of Valentina walking toward the pool with Ric. Her long legs and the way she filled out her white one-piece bathing suit knocked the wind out of him. She walked down the steps into the pool and put Ric on his back on the other raft.

Giovanni pulled the raft over to her. "I told you guys this was going to be fun."

The babies were so shocked by what was

happening, they forgot to cry. Valentina saw their expressions and laughed so hard it infected him. From the beginning they'd shared the same sense of humor. It was just one of the many things he loved about her. If there was heaven on earth, this was the place.

The next half hour of play was pure delight. As long as the babies could see both of them, they were mesmerized. Valentina had put him in the same condition. When he saw those eyes glittering like sapphires above the water as she watched him, he almost had a heart attack.

He swam over to her. "What do you say we take them in and feed them?"

"I was just going to suggest it. One dark head and one blond. Aren't they adorable?"

Giovanni's emotions were running all over the place. He grabbed Ric while she reached for Vito. Together they took the babies inside and up the stairs. Then she carried Vito and headed for the nursery in the pants and top she'd worn earlier. Giovanni had slipped into his room to put on shorts and a shirt.

They sat down and fed the babies. Ric finished first. His eyes were closed as Giovanni placed him in the crib with the fish mobile and turned it on. Very soon after Vito had finished, too. As she left the nursery to put him down, she said in a hushed voice, "We'll have to get a mobile for Vito so he won't feel left out."

"Shall we drive into town and get one? While Stanzie and Paolo keep watch, let's eat dinner out."

"Maybe we shouldn't leave the children yet."

"We won't be gone long, and I'm the one starving now."

"So am I," she confessed. "Give me a minute to change into something more appropriate."

Valentina freshened up and decided to wear one of her sundresses with cap sleeves in a pale pink. She met him at the Maserati parked at the side of the villa where a garden of white moonflowers gave off a beguiling scent.

"I feel like I'm wandering in a fantastic dream." Her eyes had fastened on Giovanni. He looked incredible in charcoal trousers and a silky dark vermilion sport shirt. Open at the neck, she could see the dark hairs on his well-defined chest. She wanted to be in his arms so badly it was killing her.

"I'm taking you to my favorite restaurant at

a hotel where Grieg stayed during his travels here. It's rumored he never wanted to leave Ravello."

"Of course he didn't. I adore Grieg. During my pregnancy I must have listened to his first piano concerto dozens of times."

He drove them out to the main road past flowered terraces and hanging gardens to the village center and pulled into the parking area reserved for the hotel patrons. Twilight had descended.

The maître d' showed them out to a patio with candlelit tables overlooking the spectacular villa gardens. Sculptured topiary trees surrounded the fountain playing below. The sight took her breath. Grieg's music, "Wedding Day at Troldhaugen," could be heard in the background, adding to her sense of entrancement.

Giovanni's eyes gleamed like jet between black lashes as he reached for her hand across the table. "Will you let me order for you?"

"I'd love it."

"Some women wouldn't like that."

"I'm not some women."

"No, you're not." He squeezed her hand before letting it go.

Soon they were feted with swordfish *pic-*

cata, a dish wrapped in ham and roasted almonds. The sumptuous meal came with kale, polenta and risotto.

After one bite, she exclaimed, "I've never tasted anything so delicious. The presentation looks too good to eat, but I plan to devour everything anyway."

Giovanni's laughter warmed her heart. They lingered over the predessert and the dessert served at the end with coffee. She passed on the wine, too drunk on the atmosphere with a man like Giovanni to get any more euphoric, but he fed her the last chocolate petit four. Her lips tingled as they brushed his fingers, causing her to hunger for his kiss.

Quite a few of the diners who recognized him nodded and stopped to shake hands. He introduced Valentina, but made no explanations about her. One of the men who'd come to their table assessed her in a way that made her blood curdle. Giovanni noticed and cut the other man off. The gossip would already be starting, but Giovanni didn't worry about lighting his own fires and made no excuses.

Female heads turned everywhere they walked. His striking features, not to mention his tall, well-honed physique made her the envy of the evening. With hands clasped, they strolled through the winding alleyways filled with flowers and shops. Valentina had reached a new high with this incredible man.

Before they left the town, they visited a children's shop. The young woman at the counter where they bought a mobile and some toys for the boys to chew on couldn't take her eyes off Giovanni.

Before heading back to the car, they stopped at another shop for two bottles of *limoncello*, a favorite product in this land of lemons. "One of these is for Paolo and Stanzie. The other is for us."

"I had it once years ago."

"From the lemons here in Ravello?"

"I'm sure not."

"Then you're in for a treat. Tonight is a special occasion. After we get home, I thought we'd drink a toast to our time together. May it last."

If only that were possible.

Right now Valentina couldn't relate to the life she'd led before meeting Giovanni. She felt like she'd been brought to an enchanted mountain by a prince right out of a fairy tale. Everywhere she looked, bursts of flowers in every color hid exquisite villas and palazzi. Cypress trees formed picturesque silhouettes against the night sky. From dizzying heights she looked down the many sloping gardens to the sea and breathed in the delightful fragrance of citrus and rose.

But the most tantalizing fragrance of all came from the soap Giovanni used, combined with his own male scent. She was drawn to it the way a bee zoomed in on an orange blossom, wanting its nectar, the food of the gods.

He could be a Roman god, but she was thankful he wasn't. Otherwise he wouldn't have brought her to dinner or fed her dessert from his own hand. The contact had sent spirals of desire through her body.

As they reached the villa, she noticed a thumbnail moon climbing in the velvet sky. "This has been a perfect day and a perfect night, Giovanni."

"Almost perfect," he muttered. "I'm sorry Claudio made you uncomfortable. He's a gossip, and he's known as a womanizer, who wished he'd been the one sitting next to you tonight."

"Please don't apologize for his behavior. It—"

"It happens all the time?" he finished her words. "I know. A man wouldn't be a man if he didn't notice you. I'm the lucky one."

She sucked in her breath. "You're very good for a woman's ego. Thank you for tonight. It's one I'll never forget." She heard her own voice quiver from emotion.

"It's not over yet."

They went inside the sunroom. "Stay here. I'll get two aperitif glasses." He took one of the *limoncello* bottles with him.

She put their sack of purchases down on the table while she waited.

Soon he returned. "I checked on the children. They're sound asleep. Stanzie and Paolo are happy with our gift and have gone off to have their own celebration." He opened the other bottle and poured them each some liqueur. She took one, he picked up the other.

"I'd like to make a toast." He stared into her eyes. "To our partnership, which I've wanted since the first day at the hospital." He clicked her glass and drank.

His admission caused her hand to tremble as she sipped her drink that looked like liquid sunshine. "Giovanni, I—"

He stopped the flow of words with a touch of his finger to her lips, fanning the flame he'd ignited at dinner. "Can you imagine a time when we won't be partners? Not every baby switch has a happy ending as we've learned after reading all the research. Our children deserve the very best from both of us. We owe it to them and each other for the rest of our lives."

She pondered what he'd said. *Partners* had been an interesting choice of words. When he'd asked her to move in, he'd said he didn't know for how long. Giovanni was used to thinking in business terms. In the metaphoric sense she agreed they'd be partners for a lifetime because of the link to the children. But in a literal sense she didn't see them staying together longer than a month.

By then Ric would have grown attached to Giovanni. Vito would be old enough for the separation, since she planned to move back to Naples to finish her studies. The winter semester would be starting in September. There were good day-care centers suggested by the university. Valentina would make inquiries and find the one that suited her best.

Thank goodness for student loans. After she graduated and got a good job with an engineering firm, she'd pay it off. Knowing that Giovanni worked in Naples, she expected he'd come to see Vito, so that bond wouldn't be broken. She'd see him and Ric from time to time. It could all work.

"I'll think about everything you've said. Thanks again for the lovely evening." She put the glass down. *Get out of here, Valentina, before you can't.* "Now I'm headed for bed."

"*Buonanotte.*"

Valentina's heart thundered in her chest all the way to her room. There'd be little sleep for her tonight. But to her surprise, she did sleep until Vito awakened for his bottle at four.

Around seven she got up and dressed in jeans and a top, expecting that Giovanni would have left for work. But when she carried Vito down the hall to the nursery, she found him feeding Ric. He was clean shaven and wore another pair of jeans and a creamy colored crewneck shirt. It didn't matter what he wore, he was a sensational-looking man.

She reached for a bottle and put it in the microwave. "Don't you need to get to your office?"

His dark gaze swept over her, making her far too aware of him. "I've arranged for some time off. How would you like to go out on my cruiser? I thought we'd visit several places and be gone for two or three nights. You can do night duty for me at some point. It's true I've been a *cavallo di battaglia* too long."

"But don't forget that being a workhorse

put you in the reins of your family's company in the first place."

"I'm not sure if I like it. Right now I find that I'm loving to be on vacation and don't want it to end."

She knew how hard he worked, but this baby had forced him to take a break. No invitation could have thrilled her more. "The boat is the perfect way to enjoy ourselves with the children without having to take them in the car."

"My thinking exactly. Unless there's anything else you need to do, we'll leave after breakfast."

They worked together to pack up the children and their things. Valentina hurried to her room to do some packing. Before long they went downstairs with all their paraphernalia to eat.

After breakfast, they packed up the car. The Brunos waved them off.

Giovanni drove along a road that wound lower and lower to a private area of beach where he kept his boat tethered to the pier.

"What a wonderful cruiser!"

"When Paolo and Stanzie moved in the villa, I told them they could take it out whenever they wanted, so they've kept it in top condition."

"It's nice to see that a couple who work together are so much in love. You can tell by their glances and smiles at each other."

"No one could ever say that about Tatania and me. The secret is to fall in love first. Those lucky enough for that to happen have love going for them when they marry."

"I'm sorry your marriage didn't work. I know you've told me it's all your fault, but I know that's not true. Did she really not know you were a hard worker? I bet if you asked her, she would have to admit she looked past that trait in you. If she could have been honest with herself, she might have decided to follow her own instincts to find a man who wasn't a workaholic."

"Hindsight is a wonderful thing."

"Don't I know it," she said with a wry smile. "If I hadn't felt like such a failure, I would have realized why Matteo had so much influence over me by telling me what I needed to hear."

He shook his dark head. "A failure? When you've almost received your graduate degree in engineering at the age of twenty-five?"

"Looking back, I realize how odd that

sounds now. But growing up, it felt like my brothers received all the attention and I admit I was jealous. My mother tried to help me. She said that one day I'd become my own person and those feelings would go away."

Giovanni stared hard at her. "Have they gone?"

"Now that I'm a mother, I've been forced to grow up. Somehow those feelings of jealousy I harbored seem absurd in light of the problems you and I have been forced to face."

He nodded. "Becoming a parent has been a life-changing experience for me, too. Work used to be everything. But since Vito was born, I can't get home to him at night fast enough."

"They are absolutely precious."

"We're very lucky."

"Yes," she whispered.

They got the children on board with the other items. Then he reached for the infant life preservers his siblings had used for their babies. After putting them on the children, they placed them in their carry-cots and lowered the visors to shield them from the sun. After undoing the ropes, Giovanni started the engine and they made their way at a wakeless speed into open water.

CHAPTER SIX

THE GULF OF SALERNO offered some of the most divine scenery imaginable. Along this winding coastline, steep rocky slopes rushed down to the sea, and tiny villages with colorful houses stacked on top of each other clung to the rugged cliffs.

Had Valentina ever been this happy? She couldn't remember.

While Giovanni piloted the boat, she walked to the rear of the fabulous cruiser, resting one knee on the banquette to watch birds and fish, along with the colorful sailboats off in the distance. Later, after lunch, they carried the babies below to one of the bedrooms for their nap. For the next few hours she and Giovanni were free to enjoy this pleasurable moment out of time.

"Since I've anchored the boat, will you be all right if I take a swim?"

"Of course."

"I'd ask you to join me."

"No. One of us has to stay on board. Go for it, Giovanni. The water is so inviting."

"I'll be right back." He disappeared below, leaving her alone to brood over the time when they had to say a real goodbye. She had to fight thoughts of one day being married to him. He'd only recently been divorced. To take on a new wife would be the last thing he'd want. Though they wouldn't be parting company for a while, her heart was already rebelling.

Giovanni emerged on deck in blue swim trunks. His hard-muscled body took her breath before he slid over the side into the water and started swimming around the cruiser with the speed of a torpedo. He circled maybe ten times, then trod water close to the end of the boat with his hair sleeked back.

She smiled at him. "You look like you're having a marvelous time."

"I haven't taken a day off like this in years."

"Neither have I."

"I'll get back on board so you can have a turn."

"I would, but I'm not ready to swim in the

sea yet. Please stay out there as long as you want. I'm enjoying watching you."

"After we go back to my place, you can use the pool so I'm able to watch *you*."

Warmth rushed to her face that had nothing to do with the sun. "I don't want to go back. This is glorious."

"Then we won't."

She drank the rest of her water. *Don't tempt me, Giovanni.* "You have a business to run."

"Didn't you hear what I just told you? Right now my only business is to love Ric and make him feel secure. With your help it's happening."

"I don't know how I would have gotten through all this without your help. Vito is a different baby."

He flashed her a smile that melted her bones. "We do good work."

Too good. Her mind told her she shouldn't have gotten involved with him once they'd left the hospital, but that wasn't what her heart was telling her.

"Ready or not, I'm coming aboard!" He swam to the end of the boat. With stunning male dexterity he heaved himself onto the transom. She handed him one of the towels so he could dry himself off. "Before the babies wake up, come and sit by me while we drive on."

She didn't need to be urged.

He threw the towel around his shoulders and took his place at the wheel. Valentina handed him his life preserver. "Please put it back on."

"For you I'll do it."

"For Ric. He's going to want you around forever."

She couldn't decipher the look in his incredible black eyes that held hers before he turned on the engine. All she knew was that once he'd raised the anchor and they'd taken off across a calm sea, a thrill of exhilaration swept through her just to be sitting next to him.

The sight of the lemon-grove terraces of the cliffs combined with the delicious scent gave her a feeling of euphoria. When she moved to an apartment in Naples, she would always remember this time with a man who was bigger than life to her. His ex-wife could roam the earth and never meet another man like Giovanni.

"What's on your mind, Valentina? Talk to me."

"I guess I'm trying to understand the other

reasons why your marriage didn't work. What else caused the strife? Ric is so dear. If your ex-wife saw him, her heart would melt."

To her surprise he brought the boat to a stop and turned to face her. "Where to start? My parents wanted me to marry her. Tatania's father, Salvatore, was in business with mine. They're both on the board of the company. Because some of my family board members wanted to champion a second cousin of mine to take over the reins, my father didn't want that to happen.

"My mother came to me in private and told me that Tatania's father wanted our marriage. He worked hard on my father to talk to me. A marriage would bring the needed votes in my favor to put me in as head instead of my cousin. Mother begged me to do this because my father was intimidated by Salvatore and always had been.

"I realized my father had always lacked a certain confidence. He looked to me to help fight all the internal battles. That bit of knowledge about his insecurity finally persuaded me to follow through."

"Are you saying she married you because of her father's pressure?"

"To some degree, yes. I'd had various girlfriends throughout my life, but nothing serious. Because of my parents' urgings, I started spending time with her and we got on well enough. Knowing my father was pinning all his hopes on my asking Tatania to marry me, I could see that if I didn't, it could break his spirit.

"But once we were married, she complained about the hours I was working. I questioned how she could be upset since she knew what my life was like. She claimed that she'd loved me from the first time she'd met me, but she didn't know what it meant to be married to a CEO.

"It's true I worked harder than I'd ever done. Both my father and hers had big expectations where I was concerned."

"How old are you?"

"Thirty-two."

"That's young to have so much responsibility."

He nodded. "I worried I would let my father down if I didn't do the lion's share. I told Tatania that if I did the hard work now, then I could slow down after a couple of years. But our home life did suffer. It got to the point that she said she didn't want to start a family if I didn't spend more time at home. I felt trapped."

"Did she have a job?"

"No. She led an active social life, but the day came when she said she was going to stay at her parents for a while. After two months' separation, we talked and decided to try again. I promised to stay home more. That worked for two weeks, but then there were new problems out of the country I had to see about. She refused to travel with me."

"Why?"

"Because it would mean her sitting in a hotel room all day long while I was working."

"She didn't like exploring new places?"

"Not alone."

"How sad."

"Tatania couldn't take any more of my being absent and filed for divorce. It's true that I was a willing pawn at the time of our marriage, but I'd intended to be a good husband. Unfortunately I didn't marry Tatania for the right reason. Without being in love with her, our marriage couldn't make it. You know the rest."

"But after she was pregnant—"

"That's the mystifying part. She said she didn't want the baby even if we stayed married because then she'd be stuck raising her baby by herself because I wouldn't be around. She had every reason to believe that was true. Tatania was also convinced that another man wouldn't look at her if she had a baby in tow. As you can see, I did damage to our marriage and she became embittered."

"I'm sorry I brought up something that's so painful for you."

"Not painful anymore. Just sad. I've been thinking about Vito's father, who hasn't stayed in touch with you if only to know he had a son."

"A baby would ruin his lifestyle. He wants his pleasures without any of the responsibility. The man never grew up." She stared at him. "The past is behind us, Giovanni. We're the lucky ones to be the parents of our wonderful babies. And guess what? I think I can hear one of them fussing. I'll go down and bring them up."

"We'll feed them and put them in the playpen."

She stood up. "I'll need to get pictures with my phone." Valentina wanted some of Giovanni to keep forever.

"I want to take pictures, too," he asserted.

Did he want one of her? Fool that she was, she hoped he did.

"See you in a minute." She could hear both of them crying now. "I'm coming!"

With the babies propped in the playpen, Valentina stretched out on her back on one of the side banquettes to get a little sun and let Giovanni drive them farther along the coast. Such a gorgeous day with only a light breeze made their outing idyllic.

He turned on some music from the iPod. Suddenly the air was filled with the sound of Pavarotti singing Italian love songs. She'd grown up on classical music and adored opera. Learning that he enjoyed it, too, added another fascinating dimension to this remarkable man.

Valentina sat up. "These love songs make me cry."

Giovanni turned off the engine and looked back at her with a satisfied expression. "I remember my mother crying over opera. It's in our Neapolitan genes, Valentina. Our family had arguments at our house over who was, or is, the better tenor—Caruso, Pavarotti or Bocelli."

She laughed. "I could add another great to that list. Mario Lanza from the American films. When I heard him sing 'Ave Maria' in the cathedral with the choir, it was so beautiful, it hurt. And after I heard Pavarotti sing 'Celeste Aida,' I felt I was listening to an angel."

Giovanni nodded. "When this is over, shall I put on the flower song he sang in *Carmen*?"

"Oh, yes! It's another aria that tears your heart apart." They looked at each other, but with him wearing sunglasses, she couldn't see what was going on in his mind. "My mother's love of classical music infected me at an early age. Her favorite opera was *Madame Butterfly.* I wasn't as enamored after I read the short story of the naval officer who used Butterfly for amusement before abandoning her."

Giovanni removed his glasses to reveal eyes filled with compassion. "You see yourself as Butterfly?"

"I didn't know I did until just now. I've lost some confidence, Giovanni."

He sat forward. "You're not alone. Tatania lost so much faith in me, she didn't want to mother our child. I was anything but the supportive husband. Over the months during her pregnancy I'd begun to doubt my ability to be a good husband, let alone a good father."

"But you're wonderful! Can't you feel it?" she cried softly.

"Meeting you is helping me find my center, Valentina. I intend to keep working on getting better at it, but you have to know my gratitude to you knows no bounds."

His confession sank deep in her heart.

He started the engine, and once more they cruised through the calm water. The late afternoon sun shone down, reminding her to turn over. She laid her head on her arms and kept an eye on the babies while she absorbed the music like a sponge.

For the next half hour she lay there entranced. When the tape ended, she got to her feet and was surprised to find they'd come to a tiny stretch of pebbled beach along the coast. He'd pulled into a dock and shut off the engine. She had to look way up to see the top of the verdant mountains. They had a magnificence that kept her in awe.

"What's this place?"

"Laurito Beach. Few people know about it. When I was young, my friends and I would come here in the summer and build a fort in the trees. This small cove was the starting point for the pirates who used to raid the commercial boats passing by. We pretended to be pirates. The little village of Laurito I was telling you about is higher up the mountain."

Giovanni got out and tied up the boat. "The Ristorante Da Adoni a few yards off caters to anyone, a come-as-you-are spot. I'm hungry for dinner."

She was, too. They picked up the carrycots and walked the short distance where they could eat and enjoy the view of the water. Giovanni ordered them *zuppa di cozze*, a soup of mussels freshly caught, followed by *coniglio all'Ischitana*, an exotic rabbit dish with garlic, chilli, tomato, herbs and white wine. Divine, divine.

They both held the babies on their laps while they ate. The waiter grinned at them. "So nice to see the *mamma* and *papà* out together with the *bambini*." He whispered something to Giovanni she didn't catch. After he walked away, she asked what he'd said.

"You'll blush."

"Oh, dear."

"But you want to know, right?"

Valentina chuckled.

"I thought so. He said how lucky I was that I had such a delicious-looking wife when she'd just given me two babies. What joy to make another one with her right away!"

That *did* make her blush. "You made that up."

He lifted his hands. "I swear."

If he'd take off his sunglasses, she'd be able to see if he was kidding her.

"He said something else, too, but then you'd turn red like a lobster."

"Thank you for editing his remarks."

Giovanni's low laughter resonated inside her. "Did you know the Ravello summer music festival is putting on a performance of Wagner's *Parsifal* near the end of August? I don't know who the tenor will be, but I'll get front-row tickets for us whether it's held indoors or outside."

To see that with Giovanni would be another thrill of a lifetime. The thrills were stacking up minute by minute. Though she would probably be in Naples by that date, she kept the thought to herself. Valentina didn't want to spoil their time together during this trip.

"You do too much. I can never repay you."

"Our relationship isn't based on payment."

"I know. But I still want to thank you for your unending generosity." Time to change the subject. "Where are we headed next, Captain?"

A smile broke out on his tanned face.

"There's another cove five minutes away where we'll anchor for the night."

After they carried the babies back to the boat, they took them downstairs to get them ready for bed. Then Giovanni went up on deck to drive the boat to the spot where they would spend the night. As he was lowering the anchor, his cell phone rang.

He'd put it in a dashboard compartment. After reaching for it, he checked the caller ID. His father knew he'd taken some time off. He wondered what reason had prompted him to call while Giovanni was on holiday.

He clicked on. "Papà?"

"Quanto tempo, figlio mio."

It hadn't been that long since they'd seen each other. This call was about something else.

"What's the problem?"

"Claudio told me he saw you out dining last night with a very beautiful blonde woman. She's Vito's *mamma*, so don't deny it."

"I'm denying nothing. She's with me now."

"Tatania's family is outraged that you've brought that woman into your house."

His father misspoke. Only Salvatore was upset because it interfered with his plans to get Tatania back with Giovanni. "It's my business surely. Our divorce was final months ago and don't forget, she divorced me."

"They're suing the hospital. When you file suit, too, the publicity won't be good if you're involved with the Montanari woman."

Ah. Now his father had gotten to the point. "I have no intention of suing the hospital."

"Of course you will. This should never have happened."

"Valentina and I talked it over. It was a terrible mistake, but there was no malice in what happened. Therefore there's no justification in suing anyone. Since Tatania refused to see the baby after it was delivered, the switch meant nothing to her. Papà, you know full well that this is all coming from Salvatore and *not* Violeta, who is a reasonable woman and loves my birth son.

"As for Valentina and me, we've rectified the situation to our satisfaction. Now we're involved in helping our babies adjust to the switch. It's working beautifully."

"Giovanni—" He lowered his voice. "Putting the suit aside, the Montanari woman was never married. Everyone's talking about the sister of Rinieri Montanari who got pregnant out of wedlock by that amorous professor from the university. It doesn't look good for my son who's the CEO of Laurito's to be seen in her company. Your judgment should be beyond reproach."

"That's too bad, Papà, because she has moved in with me. We and the babies are very happy. I'm on vacation and won't be back in the office for a couple of days. We'll talk then if you wish. I love you and Mamma. *Ciao*."

Valentina was standing by him when he clicked off. His eyes swerved to her. "How much did you hear?"

"It's started, hasn't it? That man who stopped at our table last night, the one who kept undressing me with his eyes? He's already gone running to your father."

Giovanni nodded. Claudio might be married, but he had other women on the side. The way he'd looked at Valentina had disgusted him. "We knew this kind of trouble had to happen and have already discussed it."

"But I know you love your father," she persisted, "and you don't want to disappoint him."

"I know you love yours, but no one else is involved in this except you and me and our children."

She moistened her lips nervously. "It could get ugly for you."

"I won't let it. We're partners, remember?"

"How could I possibly forget?"

"Good. That's what I wanted to hear. Now let's go downstairs to bed."

He set the boat alarm and they went below. She changed into a pair of navy sweats he loved. Both children slept in their carry-cots in his cabin. When she would have gone to the other cabin, he said, "Stay in here with me tonight, Valentina. The queen-size bed is perfect for us. This way I can guard the three of you with no worry."

Without waiting for her response, he swung her up in his arms and laid her down on the bed. "I might want to have my way with you, but only with your permission."

"Not in front of the children," she teased, but she stayed right there. "Where are you taking us tomorrow?"

"We'll travel along the coast to the medieval village of Castellabate. It's a World Heritage Site. Later in the day we'll take the children ashore in their strollers so we can explore the small streets and alleys. You'll love it. And if we're up to it, we can walk to the thirteenth-century castle at the top for a spectacular view."

"I've never been there before."

"I seem to remember a restaurant that serves the best calamari and saffron risotto with porcini you ever tasted. My mouth is watering just thinking about it."

"One would think that's all you have on your mind."

"That's how much you know." Without hesitation, Giovanni brushed her mouth briefly with his own. He'd been needing to do that or go out of his mind. She kissed him back, then turned to face the babies.

"Where did you go?" he whispered against her neck.

"This is happening too fast."

"But I want to do it, again and again. Don't tell me you didn't like it because I wouldn't believe you."

His declaration was like a bolt of lightning penetrating her body. "I did like it. That's not the point."

"Then what is?"

"I've been attracted to you from the first day we met, and it frightens me."

"Why?"

"I never felt this way about Matteo. This is so different. I know my love for the babies has a lot to do with the strength of my feelings for you. What I can't figure out is how to separate what's really going on inside of me. All I know is, I'm a mom now and I need to concentrate on that without letting personal feelings complicate everything. Let's go to sleep."

"I'll try," he murmured.

The children woke up once in the middle of the night. They fed them in bed, then put them back in their carry-cots. Once all was quiet, he pulled Valentina against him and buried his face in her hair. "Don't think of moving away from me. Not now, not ever."

"You mustn't keep saying things like that to me."

"I can't help it. I didn't have a mad passion for Tatania. I'm afraid *you* take the honors in that department."

She squeezed her eyes together. "It's because I'm Vito's mom. You're reading too much into it."

"I agree it's because of that and a myriad of intangibles. But I can hear your next argument. Both of us have come out of unsatisfying relationships and being together is filling a void. I can add several others. I need the woman who mothered Ric for two weeks to become his nanny so I can go to work without worry. And you're a Montanari. Binding our two families will build a dynasty and—"

"Stop!"

"Relax, Valentina. We're partners. Until you want to touch me so much you can't stay away from me, I'll keep my hands and mouth off you."

Valentina lay there awake for a long time. Giovanni was a man of strong feelings and instincts that had propelled him to the kind of success most men could only dream of. To tell her he was madly attracted to her had to be an exaggeration. It was probably more of the idea that he was happy after being unhappy for so long. That described her state of mind. He'd created this fantasy world.

With the children being so content now, everything seemed perfect. It would stay that way until the real world intruded. The phone call from his father was only the beginning. Before long she'd be hearing from her family. Pretty soon everything would fall in on them, but until that happened she wanted to stay here in his arms.

When the babies started fussing, she fed them and went to the galley to make break-fast. Giovanni loved food. Because of his energy, he didn't gain weight. A little while later she called him to come and eat.

They ate at the pull-down table while the babies watched from their carry-cots. He acted so happy and was so much fun to be with, she never wanted this vacation to end. When they finished eating, she cleaned up the kitchen while he took the babies up on deck.

Their day turned out to be glorious, but the climb to the castle at the top wore her out. After a delicious fish dinner in the town, it felt good to get back to the cruiser and relax. Before long it was time to feed the babies and put them to bed.

Giovanni flashed her a compelling smile. "Now that we're alone, how about a game of *tressette*? Sit on the banquette by me." He produced a deck of cards.

Valentina eyed him with a smile. "I don't think I've played it."

"I'll teach you."

Once they got going, she didn't want to stop. "I'm going to beat you if it kills me!" But she never did and he chuckled with absolute glee. "You're cheating. You *have* to be!"

"I swear I'm not."

"Let me see your cards." Something was wrong. "Show me the palm of your hand."

He stared at her through veiled eyes. "Now, why would I do that?"

"You *are* cheating!" She grabbed his hand, but he was so strong she couldn't pry his fingers apart. Laughter rolled out of him despite her frustration. "You're terrible!" She tried again and found her shoulder against his chest.

His free arm went around her and pulled her closer. "I lied," he murmured near her ear. "I'm sorry, but you're so much fun I couldn't help myself." He undid his other hand so she could see cards he'd kept hidden. "Forgive me?" he asked and released her.

She felt his warm breath on her cheek, increasing her desire for him. To her chagrin she didn't want him to let her go.

Until you want to touch me so much you can't stay away from me, I'll keep my hands and mouth off you.

Valentina had been the one to start this intimate tug-of-war. She'd reached for his hand, not the other way around. Aware that she'd given herself away, she got up from the banquette. "It's time to check on the children."

Giovanni followed her below and they got ready for bed. Valentina looked down at them. "They're so sweet. I never knew how much I would love being a mother."

Giovanni lounged against the door. "I'm still reeling from the joy of fatherhood. I felt a deep sadness when Tatania told me she didn't want anything to do with it once she'd had the baby. But neither she nor Matteo could have any comprehension of what they're missing."

She turned to him. "I'm not sorry for what we're doing. We owe them everything we can do to give them the best start in life, even if the world says scathing things about us."

"Your children have a warrior for a mother. It's a privilege to know you, Valentina. Now let's get in bed."

His words stayed with her long after he'd wrapped his arms around her. Giovanni had a way of making her feel cherished. If she'd never met him, she would never have realized a man like him was out there in the cosmos. Twenty-eight thousand baby switches a year worldwide. What were the odds of it happening to her and Giovanni?

The next day they headed toward home. En route they went ashore at several places for a meal. Giovanni swam while she took pictures of him. By evening they'd cruised close to Ravello, but anchored near the pier to spend one more night on board. Once the babies were down, he turned on another Pavarotti track.

Valentina wanted to prolong this moonlit night because tomorrow he'd have to go to work. It wouldn't just be the babies who would miss him. But he would always come home at the end of the day because he was a devoted father.

She lay down on her stomach on one of the banquettes. "Could we sleep up here tonight? It's glorious out. We'll keep the doors open to listen for the children."

"You're reading my mind." He walked over and threw a light blanket over her. She watched him lie down on the banquette opposite her. They turned to each other, supporting their heads with their arms. "Have you ever gone camping?"

"No. Carlo used to go and I'd beg him to take me. He'd always say, 'next time.'"

"Would it interest you to go with me?"

"I can't think of anything I'd like more. We'd carry the babies on our backs in those fun-looking pouches. You're talking a campfire and a tent, right?"

Giovanni sat up suddenly. In the darkness, the sight of his arresting features excited her to the core. "Where did you come from?" His voice sounded husky.

"I've been wondering the same thing about you."

"Some of my happiest memories were out camping and fishing with my friends. I want to teach the boys to love the outdoors."

"Whenever you want to go, I'm your man."

A broad smile broke out on his handsome face. "What a man!"

She laughed.

"Being with you makes me want to become a house dad so we can do everything together."

"That would work for about a week, then you'd need the stimulation of applying that amazing brain of yours to the business you love. My mother understood that about my father. She was a very smart woman."

"You must miss her a lot."

"Oh, I do. She would have loved Vito and teaching me how to be a good mother."

"Trust me, Valentina. You already are because you've put his happiness before your own. That takes a very special person. If she were alive, she'd be tremendously proud of you."

His praise caused her throat to swell. "I

could say the same thing about your fatherly virtues, even if you do love business."

"I love exploring new markets, but not the administrative duties."

"Well, your company is depending on you to go on doing great things for them."

"What about you?"

"I've made up my mind to take classes this winter semester to finish my degree."

After a long silence, he said, "You can fly to Naples with me on the days you have classes. I'll fly you home after."

She raised herself up on one elbow. "Giovanni? You and I *will* be partners forever. But when I told you I'd live with you, I didn't mean forever and neither did you. Once August is over, the boys will be better able to handle the separation. I'm planning to find an apartment in Naples near the university and put Vito in day care attached to the university. I'll always want you to come by and bring Ric, but I need to make my own way."

His brows furrowed. "If you're thinking of doing this to protect my reputation, then forget it, Valentina."

"Giovanni—this isn't about you. It's about me becoming independent. The women in the Montanari family don't have careers. I'll be the first."

"You can do that. I'll help you."

"That's the problem. I've been helped all my life. Now that I have a baby, I need to do this by myself."

"How will you finance everything?"

"A student loan. If I'm careful, I can get through school. After that I'll find a job and pay it back like thousands of other husband-less women do. You have no idea how much it would mean to me to make something of my-self. Rini and Carlo have done it. So can I."

"Your brothers got help, too. With your name being Montanari, the university won't give you a loan."

"You're probably right, so I'll apply under my mother's maiden name."

"That's illegal. If you need a loan, I'll give you one."

She slid off the bench. "You're a man in a million, Giovanni. I've always been given help, and now here you are offering to pay my expenses so I can finish school. As if I'd let you do that. I *have* to do this by myself, even if I have to get an entry-level job first and take another couple of years to get my degree. Please tell me you understand."

He exhaled slowly. "I do. You're the woman born with the proverbial silver spoon in your mouth. My admiration for you just keeps growing because you want to make your own way."

Valentina hadn't expected an answer like that. He always had a way to distill a potential problem. "Thank you for taking me seriously and for offering to help me financially." She took another drink of water, then lay back down.

"You're welcome. How soon are you going to look for a job?"

"In a couple of weeks."

"Good. Then let's forget those plans and enjoy the time we have together. How does that sound?"

Giovanni was being so kind and agreeable she hardly knew what to say. "I don't deserve your kindness."

"*Deserve* is an odd word. Why do you use it?"

She bit her lip. "I went against the principles I was brought up with by getting involved with Matteo. If I try hard to be the best mother and provider I can be for the rest of my life, then maybe I'll be able to forgive myself."

"That's a lot of guilt you're carrying around. I'm sure your family doesn't make you feel that way. You're an amazing woman. You need to be kind to yourself."

"Thank you for saying that. You're a terrific listener. It explains why your family looks to you for leadership."

"I've noticed you have trouble accepting a compliment. You'd better get used to it because as I told you, I've never been so attracted to a woman."

This wave of euphoria with the children would pass for him. However Valentina feared her attachment to him went much deeper than that. She buried her face in her arms until she knew no more.

CHAPTER SEVEN

VALENTINA PROPPED THE babies in their swings by the pool while she looked for a job on her laptop. Since Giovanni had taken them down the coast on the cruiser two weeks ago, the time had flown by and she needed to get busy.

He'd gone to work each business day, but had come home early to play with the children. They'd settled down to a routine and last weekend had spent time touring the grounds of the Villa Cimbrone, for which Ravello was famous.

Their long walks and talks while they enjoyed the babies had been heavenly. But pretty soon she needed to register for school *if* she was going to go at all.

"Valentina?" She looked up to see Giovanni walking toward her. "I missed you at breakfast. What's going on?"

She was always so thrilled to see him, she

could hardly breathe. "I got up early to look for a part-time job that will fit with my studies."

"I'm glad you're going ahead with your plans."

"You really mean that?"

"Of course. I know how important getting that degree is to you. Have you decided where you want to live?"

"I've already found an apartment online, but I need to see it in person and visit the day-care center I have my eye on. Rini told me he'd give me enough money until I receive my first paycheck from the job. Then I'll pay him back."

"Good for you."

"Giovanni—you have no idea how much your support means to me." Her voice caught. "You've done everything for me and I've done nothing in return."

"What are you talking about?" He gripped her upper arms, pulling her out of the deck chair. Lines had darkened his face. "You've helped me transition from being a robot into a flesh-and-blood human being and father. I couldn't have done any of this without you. Don't you understand?"

He pressed a kiss to her lips and shook her

gently before his hands slid away with seeming reluctance. The contact sent her pulse racing. "A-are you leaving now?" she asked, her voice faltering.

"Yes. I'll see all of you after I get home from work and we'll talk some more about your plans." He acted like he wanted to say more, then changed his mind and walked back in the house. Before long she saw the helicopter fly off, taking her heart with him.

No sooner had he gone than she heard a voice. "Valentina?" She turned her head in time to see Giovanni's mother-in-law walking toward her.

"Violeta—how nice to see you." Both she and Giovanni's mother had come by twice in the past two weeks. Valentina had missed her mother horribly and enjoyed both women's company.

"The babies are adorable, but it's you I need to talk to."

"Please sit down, Violeta. How are you?"

"I need to tell you something because I know you are a good person and a wonderful mother."

Valentina's brows broke into a delicate frown. "I think the world of you, too. What's wrong?"

"If my husband knew I was here to tell you this, he'd have grounds to divorce me. The mood he has been in since the baby switch has been very hard on me."

"Why has it upset him so much?"

"He's convinced that if it hadn't happened, Giovanni would have been to see Tatania by now and help her to get better emotionally."

"I see." Knowing how Giovanni really felt made this uncomfortable for Valentina.

"Giovanni's preoccupation with both babies has changed him. His mind isn't on the pressures of his position as CEO. He told me he has no intention of suing the hospital for the mishandling of the babies. For that decision my husband blames you for living in this house and your influence over him."

She shook her head. "I have no influence, Violeta. He loves both babies. That love has prompted him to make certain decisions. I—I love both babies, too," she confessed. "This has been hard on everyone. We're trying to do the right thing."

"Nevertheless my husband has been in conference with Giovanni's father, and there's a groundswell from the board to ask Giovanni to step down as CEO. Were you aware of that?"

"No—" Valentina clutched the edge of the table. She felt like she'd been shot. "But you can go home and tell your husband he has nothing more to worry about. I'll be living in Naples by the end of the week."

"You mean at Giovanni's apartment there?"

Valentina knew he kept one, but he'd never pushed it on her. He understood she wanted to be independent. Something about his calm, caring demeanor made her want to do things his way.

"No. Winter semester is starting at the university. I'll be living nearby in an apartment I've found and putting Vito in day care. I hope to graduate in the spring and get a job."

"You're going to work?"

"Yes. I plan to be an engineer like my brothers."

"Oh—" She looked shocked. "You must be very brilliant."

"I wish." She'd never felt she could measure up to her brothers, but having given birth to Vito had given her a new sense of self-worth, never mind that Giovanni had contributed to that feeling. "But the point is, I'm convinced that the babies are happy now and that they'll be able to handle the separation so Giovanni and I can get on with our lives."

She stared at Valentina through eyes reflecting torment. "So you and Giovanni—?"

"We're not lovers, Violeta," she answered the unasked question. "We're friends who've been through a terrible ordeal and are doing our best to work things out."

Violeta looked downcast. "I'm sorry. I didn't mean to pry."

"It's all right. Giovanni loves you and loves it that you're Ric's grandmother."

Her brown eyes filled with tears. "Thank you. I love him, and I love both your babies."

Now Valentina was weepy. "They're hard not to love."

"You're easy to love, too." Valentina hadn't expected that confession from Tatania's mother. "No matter what you say, I see it in Giovanni's eyes."

"What you see is a man who has fallen in love with fatherhood." He was still in that state of euphoria, and it made his gorgeous black eyes shine. "In that respect he's unique."

"I agree," she whispered and got up from the table. "I'm going to tell my husband what you said. It will give him hope that Giovanni and my daughter will get a second chance." Valentina's heart sank, but it wasn't her place to disabuse the older woman. "I know it will stop all the talk over asking Giovanni to step down."

Valentina kept a smile on her face. "That's good for the Laurito company. Now, why don't you stay for a while. You can feed Ric his bottle."

"You'd let me?"

"Of course. He loves his *nonna*."

Violeta walked around and gave her a kiss on the cheek. "I'll come again, but your news is too important. I need to get back home and talk to my husband."

Valentina walked her to her car. When she'd disappeared, Valentina found Stazie in the sunroom putting flowers in a vase.

"Stazie? I need to fly to Naples. I know this is a great imposition, but could you tend the boys until I get back? Giovanni might get home first. I'm just not sure."

"Of course I'll tend them. You rarely let me help."

"Thank you so much."

She hurried back out to the children and phoned Rini. Luckily he was in his office. "Rini? Could I ask a great favor?" So much for her independence.

"Of course. How are you?"

"I'm ready to check out the apartment and

the day-care center. Could you send the helicopter here?"

"You mean now?"

"If it's convenient. I'll fly to your office. From there I'll get a taxi and check out those places. Maybe you can drop me back here this evening?"

"Tell you what. I need a break. When you arrive I'll ask my driver to take us where you need to go. We'll have dinner with Papà before we leave Naples."

"You're the best, Rini."

"Hey—I've missed you and Vito. I bet he's gained ten pounds since the last time I saw him."

She chuckled. "Not quite. Love you."

While she waited for the helicopter, she brought the babies into the sunroom and put them on the floor on a quilt. It was hard to leave them, but this was an emergency.

At 6:30 p.m. Giovanni jumped down from the helicopter, anxious to be with Valentina. He would ask Stanzie and Paolo to watch the children while he took her to a great restaurant for a night of dinner and dancing.

He'd kept his distance over the past two weeks. But while he'd been at work today, his thoughts had been totally focused on her. After the close quarters they'd shared on the cruiser, he'd go mad if he didn't get her into his arms.

This time of evening he usually found her in the sunroom with the babies. Instead he discovered Ric and Vito in the kitchen. Stanzie had put them in their swings while she cooked dinner. He smiled at her and kissed the boys. "Is Valentina upstairs?"

"No. She flew to Naples. Her brother will bring her home tonight."

That revelation sucked all the air out of him. "Any other news?"

"*Sì*. Signora Corleto came over this morning."

Uh-oh. "What time did she come?"

"About eleven."

"What time did Valentina leave?"

"Around noon. Dinner will be ready in a few minutes."

"Thank you, Stanzie. I'm going to take the boys for a short walk." He put them in their strollers and left the villa.

Whatever conversation had gone on between Valentina and Violeta, it had prompted his houseguest to take off. She didn't have to tell Giovanni her schedule, but the fact that he hadn't heard from her let him know something had alarmed her.

Violeta was not a vindictive woman. Quite the opposite. "Hey, guys—we're on our own until Valentina comes home." He kissed their heads. "Let's go back and eat. Stanzie has made something that smells good."

Later that night after giving them a bath and putting them to bed, he started down the stairs just as Valentina was coming up. In the dim light her classic features and gleaming blond hair emphasized her beauty.

"Welcome home," he said in a quiet voice.

"Sorry I'm late."

"You don't owe me any explanation. Stanzie told me where you'd gone."

She nodded. "After Rini and I returned to the villa, he drove me here. How are the children?"

"I put them down. Why don't you tell me about your day?"

He walked with her to the nursery. After she peeked at the boys, they tiptoed out of the room and went back downstairs to the sunroom. The night called to him. She must have felt it, too, and followed him out to the garden, where the roses were in full bloom.

She leaned over to smell one. "Their scent lies heavy on the air."

"My parents have a garden in Naples, but the fragrance here is much more powerful." His gaze wandered over her. "Did you accomplish a lot today?"

"Yes. Rini went with me. I like the apartment I'm going to rent, and I was impressed with the people who run the day-care center. They only allow ten children. Two of the four workers look solely after the babies. Both have had nursing experience. I'm sure Vito will get the attention he needs."

"Have you had success finding a job?"

"Not yet, but I'm hopeful. Rini and I had dinner with my father. It was a good day."

"I heard that Violeta dropped by."

"Yes."

"Want to tell me what you two talked about, or was it confidential?"

"She said her husband is suing the hospital."

"We already knew that. What else did she say that caused you to leave so fast?"

She turned to the view of the sea. "Whatever we talked about is no longer important."

"Why? Because you're going to move to Naples, therefore you're no longer a threat?

I'm not unaware that Tatania's parents would like us to get back together. With you out of my villa for good, that removes the biggest roadblock to effecting a reconciliation. Am I right?"

"Yes."

Giovanni grasped her shoulders and pulled her back against his chest. He buried his face in her hair and felt her tremble. "When I got home from work, I was planning to take you out for a night of dinner and dancing."

"At this point that would be a mistake."

"Explain what you mean." He turned her around. Their mouths were only centimeters apart.

"I can't. You're holding me too close to think."

After expelling his breath, he let go of her, but it took all his strength to do so. "Is that better?"

She backed away from him. Her shimmering blue eyes held a haunted expression. "Did you know there's a movement within your company to ask you to step down as CEO because everyone believes you and I are lovers?"

His blood ran cold. "Violeta *told* you that?"

"Yes, but she didn't say it in a mean way.

We like each other. She wanted me to know the truth because she loves you and Ric. I allayed her fears by letting her know that you and I are not lovers. Furthermore I told her I'm moving to Naples by the weekend."

Maybe *he'd* misjudged the situation. "In other words, you don't have deep feelings for me."

"Of course I do," she practically shouted at him.

"But it seems not deep enough, otherwise you wouldn't have flown to Naples the moment Violeta stopped by to give you the bad news. I thought we were going to do this together. Like partners, remember?"

Valentina shook her head. "We've been through all this. You knew I was planning to leave. What she told me helped me to get on with my plans a little sooner. Giovanni—you're not just anybody. You're the head of the Laurito Corporation.

"I knew we'd have to face a lot of bad publicity while we tried to do the right thing for our babies. But what I didn't know was that the board would actually remove you from your position. You've worked so hard for everything you've achieved. I refuse to be the woman who brings you down."

"Tatania's father worked on Violeta to get his own way before she showed up here. Surely you must see that."

"All I know is, I can't stay here any longer. I'm trying to put away the guilt I suffered over my bad judgment with Matteo. But if I thought that you could be toppled by your own board members because of me, terrible guilt would consume me. This is all my fault. If I hadn't asked the hospital for a DNA test, we wouldn't know of each other's existence."

His anger flared. "If you hadn't followed your mother's intuition, we wouldn't have the joy of loving two sons. Can you honestly stand there and tell me you're sorry for discovering the truth?"

"You know I'm not," her voice shook, "but I don't want to be the one responsible for ruining your life! Violeta's visit was a blessing in disguise. Just so you know, I'm going to pack everything up tonight. Rini is going to come for me and Vito in the morning. I'll stay with him until Friday. The furnished apartment will be ready then, and he'll help me move."

Blind with anger over what was happening, he knew he had to get away from her in order to calm down. Gutted by the sudden change in their arrangement, he needed to channel his negative energy with action.

"Don't let me keep you, Valentina. *Buonanotte*."

He raced back inside to his room and changed into his trunks. A good dozen laps in the pool wouldn't take away the rage he was feeling over Tatania's father. He'd always been the ultimate manipulator orchestrating everyone's lives, including Giovanni's father. But the physical exercise would help Giovanni clear his head before he put his plan into action and fought fire with fire.

When the next morning came, he purposely stayed in the bedroom so Valentina could feed the babies and say her goodbye to Ric before Rini Montanari came for her. From the other guest room window at the end of the hall, he saw her get in the car with Vito and drive away.

Now that she'd gone, Giovanni contacted his pilot, who would be picking him up within a few minutes. He'd called for a morning meeting of the entire Laurito board. For the occasion he'd dressed in a formal suit and tie.

On his way out, he stopped in the sunroom, where Stanzie was entertaining Ric in his swing. She looked up.

"You just missed Valentina."

"We said good-night last night." He leaned over to kiss his son. "I'll see you this evening."

"Is everything all right?"

Giovanni smiled at her. "Things couldn't be better."

"But…she said she was moving to Naples."

"That's right. She had a lot on her mind today. Don't worry about it."

Stanzie frowned at him. "I don't like it. Paolo and I enjoy her very much."

"She holds you two in the highest regard. I'll check in with you later to see how Ric is doing."

A half hour later he entered his office and checked with his assistant. "Has anyone bowed out of this morning's meeting?" It was scheduled to start in ten minutes.

"No, but your uncle Benito said he'd be a few minutes late."

He nodded. "I'll be making an announcement. When the meeting is over, I'll tell you what I want you to say to the media."

His assistant's eyes widened, but they'd worked together too long and he knew better than to question Giovanni.

"I'm headed for the conference room now." He left his office and started down the hall.

"Giovanni?" His father had just gotten off the private elevator.

"Papà—" He gave him a hug.

"I've been anxious to talk to you about something that has concerned me for the last month. After the meeting let's go to lunch."

"We'll do it."

They entered the room. Little by little most of the members of the board had taken their seats around the long oval table. As he stood to call the meeting to order, his oldest uncle came in with Tatania's father and took their places next to Giovanni's father.

"I appreciate all of you rearranging your busy schedules to attend this emergency board meeting. I wouldn't have called for it if it weren't for the most vital of reasons. After you put me in as CEO of Laurito's two years ago, I made up my mind to bring results that would satisfy your faith in me.

"But as all of you know, I became a father very recently. The birth of our son Vitiello has been the most soul-changing experience of my entire life. I say *our son Vitiello* because he was the son I took home from the hospital to raise. But three weeks later I discovered there was a mistake made at the hospital. Vitiello was not our baby.

"The courageous mother who went home with her baby realized something was wrong, and DNA tests were done. It turns out we had each other's babies. The hospital arranged for the mistake to be rectified. Our birth son, Riccardo, was returned to me, and her son, Vitiello, was returned to her. But not without a lot of agony because the bonding between parent and child took place before the mistake was caught.

"I now feel as if I'm the father of twins. I love both babies with every fiber of my being. I never knew how wonderful it was to be a father. It has crystallized my vision of the future in a new way. In order to be the kind of father my sons deserve, I'm stepping down as CEO, effective by the end of the day."

The gasps he'd expected were louder than even he had imagined. Both his father and Tatania's father looked like they'd had a coronary.

"What I would like to do is be the head of our marketing department, but that will be up to the new CEO." He eyed his second cousin, who'd been considered as the pick before Giovanni had been installed. "Never

question that my loyalty will always be to
Laurito. But it's a privilege to be a father and
I want to be there to enjoy as much of it as
possible.

"That's all I have to say. Thank you for
coming to this meeting."

He left the room and headed for his office to talk to his assistant. "You can tell the
press I've stepped down as CEO to devote
more time to my family. Between you and
me I hope to be given a lesser position in the
corporation that suits my needs." His assistant looked so crestfallen he added, "Don't
worry. If I'm given another job around here,
I'll want you with me."

Before there was a stampede to his office,
he texted his father.

Meet u at Alforno's, Papà. Come alone. We
need to have a long talk.

Valentina set up the swing in the kitchen for
Vito while she cooked dinner. Having moved
out of Giovanni's villa, she felt like part of
her had died. He'd done nothing to prevent
her from leaving. In fact he'd stayed away
while she'd gotten up this morning to feed the
babies. She'd thought he might come down-

stairs and try to persuade her not to go, but of course he didn't do that.

The only remedy to her heartache was to keep busy. She told Bianca to take the night off. Valentina would fix Rini's dinner herself. He liked her veal-filled cannelloni with white sauce, a recipe their mother often cooked.

She turned on the radio while she stuffed the pasta. Her favorite news station was RAI1, and she half listened to the Tuesday evening news. In the midst of cooking, she bent over to kiss her baby's precious face. She put the pacifier back in his mouth. "Next week I'll be taking you to the doctor for your next checkup. You're such a good eater he'll probably tell me you're getting too chubby."

Tears rolled down her cheeks to realize she wouldn't be living with Ric or Giovanni anymore. She knew he'd been upset over Violeta's visit, but he'd made it clear that he honored Valentina's decision to move out.

What did you want him to do? Take you upstairs and make love to you?

She didn't dare answer that question and put the dinner in the oven. The news was still on as she set the table for Rini.

"Today the country is stunned by the announcement that Giovanni Laurito, the dynamic CEO and entrepreneur of the Laurito Corporation, has stepped down from his position to devote more time to his family."

What?

With her heart thudding she rushed over to the radio to turn up the volume.

"The corporation's spokesman has shed no other light on the resignation, but already the announcement has negatively affected the stock market. Members of the board have declined comment at this time. But there's speculation that due to his divorce from Tatania Corleto, the daughter of Salvatore Corleto, one of the pillars of the company, certain internal domestic problems forced him to make this unexpected decision."

"No—"

"His two years as head of the corporation have shown unprecedented growth in a market that has catapulted Laurito to the top of medical machines technology throughout Europe. His reputation for—"

Valentina turned it off, not wanting to hear any more. Tears streamed down her face. "Oh, Giovanni— Look what I started—I can't bear it."

"Valentina?" She jerked around to see her brother walk in the kitchen. "What's wrong?"

"Have you heard tonight's news?"

Lines darkened his face. "It was on the noon segment. Everyone at Montanari's was surprised."

"It's my fault, Rini."

"Of course it isn't." He hugged her. "Whatever he did has nothing to do with you."

"Yes, it does." She pulled away from him. "None of this would have happened if I hadn't called the hospital about getting a DNA test."

"You can't blame yourself for wanting to know if Ric was your son!" He drew Vito out of the swing and hugged him. "Because of what you did, you have your birth son home with you."

"When I tell you what happened yesterday, you'll understand why I feel so fragmented by the news." Wiping the tears from her cheeks, Valentina recounted the conversation with Violeta.

After she'd finished, he said, "So because of what she said, you think Giovanni Laurito fell on his sword because of you?" He sounded incredulous.

"Yes! I stayed with him for a few weeks and because of that, he had to step down."

Rini shook his head. "I know enough about his character to promise you he doesn't do anything unless he wants to. He asked you to live with him for the babies' sakes. It was a joint decision, Valentina."

"I should have known better."

"Where is all this guilt coming from?"

"You know," she mumbled and walked over to the oven.

"The circumstances with Matteo were entirely different."

"When I called the university to see about classes, I found out by accident that Matteo is no longer teaching there. Because of mistakes I've made, he has gone elsewhere and now it has cost Giovanni his position at Laurito's. I'm the loose, unmarried woman who—"

"Valentina—" He cut her off. "I don't ever want to hear you talk like that again."

His anger surprised her. "What are you saying?"

"I thought you made the wrong decision to go with Giovanni, but have since changed my mind. I've seen a remarkable change in you. I'm proud of you for doing what you thought was right. Anyone can see both you and Vito are thriving. Being with Giovanni has done that for you."

"You honestly believe that?"

He nodded. "I wasn't in your skin or

Giovanni's. You both followed your intuition. Good for you."

She took the cannelloni out of the oven, hardly able to believe her ears. "If you'll sit down, I'll serve you."

He reached for Vito and sat on a chair at the table. "This little guy is worth everything you've gone through."

Valentina nodded. "I adore him." She put Rini's food and coffee on the table, then plucked the baby from his arms and sat down across from him.

"This tastes delicious. You're not eating?"

"I couldn't." She looked at him. "Rini? I'm so upset I can't think about going to school right now. A job is all I can handle. I don't want to work at a restaurant or a department store. There's an opening at one of the university bookstores. The hours are good and it's close to the apartment and the day-care center. I'm going to arrange for an interview tomorrow."

"At least that's an environment you're familiar with, but since you've decided not to go to school, there's no hurry for you to see about a job."

"Yes, there is. It's time you led your own life."

He shook his head. "I do."

"But there's more to life, brother dear. You need your privacy to make that happen. Excuse me while I bathe Vito and put him down with his bottle. Thank you for being my rock."

"I wish there were more I could do."

"If I can fly to Naples with you on Friday, I'll move in the apartment and leave Vito at the day care while I see about that job at the bookstore. I really do need to be on my own. This has nothing to do with you."

"Little sister? I've never been more proud of you than I am at this moment."

She stared at him, knowing in her heart he meant it.

In another hour she'd put Vito to bed and went to her room, but she was so racked with pain over Giovanni, she couldn't stand it any longer and phoned him. It rang a long time before going to voice mail.

"Giovanni? I—I heard the news on the radio this evening," she stammered. "Please call me when you get an opportunity. Please."

She clicked off and clutched the phone in her hand. Where was he? What was he doing? Valentina could only imagine the storm he'd created at the corporation after an announcement like that. He was so young to step down from a career of such magnitude. What would he do if he left the company outright?

Absolutely sick about it, she phoned Stanzie. They'd shared phone numbers when she'd been living at the villa in case of an emergency, but Valentina had never had a reason to call her.

Not until now...

"Pronto?"

"Stanzie? It's Valentina."

"Ah—I'm so glad it's you. His family has called and called. His *mamma* is worried sick about him."

Valentina heard the anxiety in her voice. "I tried to reach Giovanni. Where is he?"

"He came home for the baby earlier and took him out on the cruiser. They aren't back yet. By the things he took, I think maybe he'll be gone for a long time. But he shouldn't be alone, not after giving up his job." Stanzie sounded shaken. "You need to come. You are the only person who makes him happy."

"That's not true."

"I know what I see. When you came in to this house, everything changed. Why did you leave?"

She could hardly swallow. "So I wouldn't

be the one to cause trouble for him at his work."

"If his work were that important, he wouldn't have given up the position. Nothing is as important to him as the babies. You come tomorrow and Paolo will help you find him. All the time you were here, I heard you two talk like he has never talked before. Talking and laughing. He was a different person with you. Please come, Valentina. He needs you."

Stanzie clicked off before Valentina could say anything else.

He needs you.

She sank down on the side of the bed with her head in her hands. *Heaven help me. I need him.*

Quickly, before Rini went to bed, she hurried to his den, where he usually worked after dinner. She knocked on the door and he told her to come in.

He looked at her tearstained face. "What's wrong?"

"I just got off the phone with Stanzie. She says Giovanni has gone out on his cruiser with Ric and doesn't know when he'll be back. His family is terribly concerned about him. She wants me to come because she's worried, too."

Rini gazed at her through veiled eyes. "You're in love with him."

There was no hiding anything from her brother. "Yes."

"Has he told you he's in love with you?"

"No. We've never even kissed."

"Why not?"

"Because he knows how guilty I feel after what happened with Matteo. He promised me he wouldn't touch me unless I wanted him to."

"That's it?"

"No. He asked me not to leave. I did it so he wouldn't have to face the board. They were going to force him to step down because of me."

"But he was one step ahead of them and faced them anyway knowing what it would cost him. What does that tell you?"

She looked down. "I don't know exactly."

"When a man like Giovanni gives up everything for his children, it says something loud and clear. I think you know what it is. In the morning I'll fly you to Ravello so you can find out for yourself."

She couldn't credit that he was saying all this to her. "You don't think I'm terrible?"

Rini got up from his desk. "For loving a good man?"

Valentina blinked in surprise. "You think that about him?"

"I do."

"He's more than good," she cried softly. "He's the most wonderful man alive."

CHAPTER EIGHT

GIOVANNI AWAKENED TO the sound of a text. Morning had come. Ric was awake, lying there in his carry-cot on the floor in his life preserver. Giovanni picked him up to hug him and change his diaper. After that he reached for the phone.

He'd ignored all his calls and texts for the past eighteen hours. Unless it was Stanzie with some emergency, he had no desire to communicate with anyone. He looked at the screen and discovered it was Paolo.

Giovanni—come home immediately. This concerns Vito.

Just the mention of Vito caused an adrenaline rush. He texted back. What's wrong? While he waited for an answer, he got dressed in jeans and a T-shirt. When there was no response, he texted him again. I'm coming.

More anxious than ever, he freshened up, then took Ric on deck and fed him a bottle. Still no response on his phone. Why hadn't Valentina phoned him about Vito? He frantically searched all the calls and saw that she *had* phoned him late last night.

He'd made another mistake by not checking the calls until now so he could call her back. Maybe she'd taken Vito to the hospital. The thought of anything being seriously wrong with the baby made him break out in a cold sweat. He'd anchored the cruiser off Amalfi. The sea was calm. If he opened the throttle full strength, he could make it back to Ravello within a half hour.

The normally short trip seemed to take hours. Relief swamped him when he reached Ravello and slowed to a wakeless speed to pull alongside the dock. He tied the rope, then removed Ric's life preserver and lifted him to the dock in his carry-cot.

He grabbed the diaper bag. "Come on, buddy. We're going to find out what's wrong with your brother."

The drive to the villa only took a few minutes. He sprang from the car with Ric and hurried into the sunroom. "Paolo? Stanzie?"

Where in the hell were they? He raced

through the house with Ric. Maybe they were in their suite at the back of the villa, but he didn't find them. Since he knew they wouldn't leave, he decided they were upstairs for some reason and couldn't hear him.

He carried Ric with him and headed for the nursery. Before he reached the entrance, he heard the music box playing from the mobile. What on earth? He rushed in the room and caught sight of Vito in the other crib.

Giovanni set down the carry-cot and walked over to him. The baby saw him and started wiggling with excitement. "Vito—you don't look sick, thank heaven."

"He's not sick, but he *is* missing you."

Valentina's voice. He wheeled around. When he saw her, he thought he was hallucinating. "You're here—"

She smiled. "Yes. Aren't you going to pick him up? He's been waiting for you. I'm dying to hold Ric." She leaned down and pulled him into her arms. "I've missed you so much. Did you have a fun overnight with your *papà* on the cruiser?"

While she covered him in kisses, Giovanni stood there dazed. "Where are Stanzie and Paolo?"

"I gave them the rest of the day and the

night off and take full responsibility if that upsets you."

"No. They work too hard." He rocked Vito in his arms, but his eyes were a piercing black as they centered on her. "How did you persuade Paolo to text me with a message you knew would turn me inside out?"

"I honestly have no idea what he said."

"He indicated something was wrong with Vito."

"I'm sorry. When I asked them to help me find you, he said he knew how to do it."

"Paolo knows me well."

"I was cooking dinner last night when I heard about your resignation on the news. I almost fainted from shock *and* pain. To walk away from your life's work and have it go out over the news—Giovanni—when you change your mind and want to go back, the media will turn it into a circus."

The features of his handsome face were masklike. "I'll never change my mind."

She took a deep breath. "You say that now, but—"

"But nothing. While Tatania was carrying our child and refused to let me share in any of it with her, I had months to do a lot of soul-searching about my life and the things I've done wrong."

She shook her blond head. "What wrong things?"

"For starters, I should never have married her. That decision has ruined her life, but I can't do anything about that now."

Valentina moved closer to him while she held Ric. "She didn't have to marry you."

"Yes, she did. Her father had a powerful hold on her."

"Just as the love for your father persuaded you to act in a way that would make him happy."

His mouth tightened. "Our divorce has damaged her. You talk about *your* guilt, but you have no idea of mine."

"Didn't she ask for the divorce?"

"Yes."

"Did you ever have a down-to-the-bare-bones talk with her before you separated for good?"

"No. She wouldn't allow it."

"Maybe you need to find a way to reach her so you can both talk it out."

"I don't want her back, Valentina."

"I believe you, but maybe she's sorry she shut you out of her life so abruptly and wants a chance to explain why she didn't want to see the baby. Have you thought she might be too nervous to approach you after the way she cut you off?"

His head reared back. "Is that why you're here? To convince me to talk to her?" He sounded incredulous.

"Of course not," she whispered. "It hurt me that you made a decision about stepping down without telling me. I thought we were partners."

"Did it occur to you it hurt me that you left for Naples within an hour of my mother-in-law's visit? I didn't have the luxury of knowing what she'd said to you."

His remark squeezed her heart. "After the wonderful way you've treated me since we met, that was a mistake I freely confess I made. I shouldn't have gone anywhere until you knew everything. If I'd stayed put until you came home, we could have talked everything out and it might have prevented you from making a decision that is going to have a lifetime effect on you. Please forgive me."

His black brows furrowed. "Contrary to what you're thinking, my plan to step down had its genesis the moment Tatania told me she was pregnant. Long before I knew you existed, I realized that becoming a father trumped every honor the world could bestow on me. I'd been an absent husband, but I vowed I'd turn my life around and be the best father possible. Up to the end of her pregnancy, I begged her to reconsider visitation."

Valentina prayed that what she was going to say wouldn't spell the end of their relationship. "As I said, maybe you need to make one more effort. Almost six weeks have gone by. Tatania has to be feeling much better physically. I know I am. Take Ric with you. I'm sure Violeta could arrange it. She loves you and Ric. It's possible Tatania will have a change of heart and want to see your baby."

"You're serious." Again he looked astounded.

"Yes. Because of your defining moment when you found out you were going to be a father, it's possible Tatania will have that same kind of moment when she sees his precious little face. As the years go by he's going to be curious about his own mother. He'll crave her love. Think how wonderful it would be if she changes her mind and wants to be a full-time mother to him now. It could be the making of her life and Ric's.

"If she turns down the opportunity, then

you would have done everything you could and you'll be able to answer Ric honestly that you tried to do all in your power to unite mother and son."

Giovanni's gaze searched hers for at least a minute. "When did you get to be so courageous and wise?"

"When I looked in Ric's face for the first time. I didn't know he wasn't my son, but like you, I felt an overwhelming feeling of love that transcended anything else in my life. When I saw Vito for the first time, that joy doubled."

He kissed her son. "I'll think about what you've said."

"Good. Now, why don't we take the children downstairs and I'll serve us lunch. Last night I made a big casserole of cannelloni and brought it with me. Afterward we'll put the children down for their naps and talk."

"How long are you here for?"

"For as long as it takes."

His heart raced. "I thought you were moving into your apartment on Friday."

"That's still a possibility."

"But?"

"I don't know the answer yet. I'm still on vacation and I was thinking how fun it would be to drive to Laurito in your car tonight. We all want to see the town where your family came from and have dinner there. Maybe stay overnight in one of the hotels?"

"You'd better be careful what you're saying to me. I'm holding you to all of it."

"That's a relief," she tossed over her shoulder.

Valentina, Valentina... "It's high summer season. We may not be able to get separate bedrooms."

"The boys took a vote and don't see that as a problem. We're one big happy family, right?"

Excitement swept through him. If she was saying what he thought she was saying...

"As long as we're going to Laurito, I suggest we get started after lunch. There's a quaint hotel at the foot of Bulgheria Mountain in Cilento National Park. You'll love the green setting. We'll get a room right by the pool and swim tonight under the stars. How does that sound?"

"Divine."

After he took Vito downstairs to the sunroom, they put the children in the playpen. "I'm going to take a quick shower."

"Lunch will be ready when you come back down."

He paused in the doorway. "If I didn't tell you earlier, it's good to see you. Does your brother know?"

"Rini knows everything," came the cryptic response. She flashed him an intense blue glance. "It's good to see you, too. When Paolo told me he'd sent for you, I didn't know how long it would take before you came. I feared maybe you'd gone far away and wouldn't respond."

"*Vito* was the magic word to bring me back in a hurry."

"Of course. That boy changed your life and mine."

Streams of unspoken thoughts and memories passed between them before he raced up the stairs two at a time. Too much more of this emotional roller-coaster ride and his heart might not be able to stand it.

Before he headed for the bathroom, he reached for his phone and made reservations at the hotel he had in mind. A few rooms bordered the pool. The concierge said he'd arrange one for their esteemed guest Signor Laurito. Normally Giovanni didn't use his name to get what he wanted. Today was an exception because he wanted this night to be perfect.

He had one more phone call to make. Violeta picked up on the third ring. "Giovanni? Oh, how good to hear your voice. I've been out of my mind with worry over you."

"I'm sorry I haven't gotten back to you before now. How would you like to do me a favor?"

"Anything!"

"I need to sit down with Tatania and have a long talk. I'll be bringing Ric with me. Do you suppose you could arrange it without anyone else knowing? Not even Salvatore?"

After a hesitation, she said, "I'll do it. Does this mean—?"

"Violeta—" he interrupted her. "Though the divorce was final, I loved Tatania in my own way, but not the way she truly needs to be loved. I want her to marry a man who thinks the sun rises and sets with her.

"If she'll allow it, she has a son who will see her as his whole world. He needs her and she needs him. Ric already loves you."

All he heard was her weeping. Finally she said, "I'll call you tomorrow."

"Bless you, Violeta."

He hung up the phone.

And bless you, Valentina.

* * *

Valentina's breath caught when she spotted the fabulous white monastery turned resort in the middle of an enormous forest. "How big is it?"

"The forest stretches sixty thousand square meters."

"So huge! The thick pines are such a dark green, I've never seen anything like this."

"With the night falling so fast, they look almost black."

"I love it!"

With the darkening sky she could barely make out the sign as they came to the town before entering the forest.

Welcome to Laurito, with its population of a thousand souls. Its namesake is the Italian-Greek monastery established in the tenth century.

"These mountain villages are so charming, Giovanni. But you've seen all this so many times before I must drive you crazy while I gush over everything. I'm as bad as a nomad in the desert who breaks into song at the sight of an oasis."

He burst into laughter, the kind she loved

to hear because it told her he sounded happy. "How do you know so much about nomadic life?"

"One of my ancient history classes on Egypt suggested reading a true account of a nomad around 600 BC."

"Did it make you long for the desert?"

She smiled. "No. Their hardships sent shudders through me. Give me tonight's mouthwatering fish pasta dinner and the lush vegetation of these mountains any day." They drove on through the greenery until they came to the cluster of white buildings.

"We've arrived."

"I love it already."

Valentina waited in the car with the babies while he went inside to register. In another few minutes they went around to the end. When he let them inside their room with two queen-size beds, she noticed that two cribs had been set up in the corner. Giovanni had said this was a family-friendly resort.

The large window looked out on the swimming pool shaped like a giant pear. It was so close all you had to do was step out the door and dive in. Lights illuminated the water that shimmered pure aqua in the night air. A few people were out in it having fun.

She turned to Giovanni. "How did you know I've been longing for this?"

"You're not the only one."

Together they fed the babies and put them down for the night in the cribs. "Do you ever wonder if they communicate when we're not around?"

He grinned at her. "No doubt they can hear each other breathing."

"I bet it's comforting."

Giovanni kissed both of them. "I'm going to get changed and meet you in the pool."

It only took him a few seconds. After he left, she changed into her new aqua bikini. Before anything else she walked over to the cribs. Their darlings were asleep. Confident that it would be all right to leave them for a little while, she slipped out the door and stepped down into the water. Giovanni was already doing laps. With the water being the perfect temperature, she swam to the other end.

While she trod water, Giovanni's dark head emerged in front of her. "This *is* a surprise." His deep voice sent spirals of desire through her.

She loved it when he was in a playful mood. "I hoped I'd find you here."

"Did you indeed. Come here to me, darling."

No sooner had he spoken than Giovanni reached for her and drew her to the edge of the pool. He lifted her face to him. "Be very sure this is what you want."

"I want you to make love to me, but I haven't been to my doctor yet. Still, that doesn't prevent me from wanting to be close to you right now. If you don't touch me, then I'm afraid I'll be the one to die."

She heard a moan before he lowered his mouth to hers. Valentina had been wanting this for too long. She welcomed his kiss with a hunger she couldn't appease no matter how hard she tried. To be in his arms and set on fire by his passion had turned her into someone she didn't know. Every touch from him thrilled her to the marrow of her bones.

He kissed her face and neck. She did the same to him. It was as if they couldn't get enough of each other and were trying to love each other all at once. "I've been wanting to do this for weeks," he confessed.

"Then you have some idea of what it has been like for me. Whenever you've kissed the boys, I've wanted it to be my turn."

"When I look in Vito's face, I see yours. I

smell your fragrance on him. From the beginning I've suffered agony because I didn't dare make a wrong move with you. I need you, Valentina."

"Don't you know that's how I feel, too?"

His kisses grew longer, deeper. She never wanted this ecstasy to end. Then she heard a groan and he tore his lips from hers. He was literally trembling. "I don't want to do this out here where anyone can see us. Let's go inside."

She'd forgotten about the other people in the pool. Giovanni had become her entire world. With her arms around his neck, he swam them to the other end and carried her up the steps into their hotel room.

Once inside the door, he backed it closed and set her down. They didn't want to let each other go. He crushed her in his arms until there was no air between them. Those rock-hard legs trapped hers. His hands smoothed over her back and hips, igniting the woman in her. This man was everything she'd ever wanted and so much more, she was lost in a frenzy of longing that had burst out of control.

At first she thought she'd imagined the ringing of his cell phone. But when Ric started to fuss, she realized someone was trying to reach Giovanni.

He was slow to respond. "Who would be calling me this time of night?"

"You'd better answer it before both babies are awake."

Giovanni gave her a swift kiss before reaching for the phone he'd left at the bed-side table. When he sat down on the side of one of the beds to talk, she knew this was important. Taking advantage of the moment, she reached for her robe and hurried into the bathroom for a shower.

Not liking the smell of chlorine in her hair, she washed it and wrapped it in a towel. Once she'd thrown on her robe, she washed out her bikini, then walked into the other room. Something of importance was going on. He was still on the phone.

She wandered over to Ric's crib. He'd set-tled back down, thank goodness. Vito hadn't been disturbed. The sound of Giovanni's phone was familiar to the baby. That had to be the reason he'd stirred.

Valentina sat in one of the chairs and dried her hair while she waited. Her watch said ten after eleven. He kept his voice low so she couldn't make out actual words. Finally he hung up and put the phone back on the table. His head turned to her.

"Give me a minute to shower, and I'll tell you what that was about." Reality had intruded on the rapture they'd shared. It couldn't be recaptured. Not tonight. She suffered real pain. The only thing to do was counteract it.

After he disappeared, she reached for her brush to put her hair in some semblance of order and got in bed. Giovanni came back in the room a few minutes later wearing his robe. He sat on the side of her bed and reached for her hands.

"Was that your father?"

"No. Violeta. She wanted me to know that Tatania has her six-week checkup with the doctor at Positano hospital in the morning at nine thirty. She'll be driving her. Violeta believes that if I'm there with Ric waiting for her in Violeta's car when she comes out of his office, it will be the perfect time and place to talk. She'll leave the door unlocked so I can get in. Anywhere else and she might refuse to see me."

"Do you think it might be too big of a jolt for her?"

"I said the same thing to Violeta. But her

mother's instinct tells her that Tatania needs a jolt to break her out of this funk she's been in. As she pointed out, her daughter has reached rock bottom. If seeing me and the baby doesn't do anything but make her angry, then what does it matter? Tatania is already angry."

Valentina lowered her head. "A mother's instinct is a powerful thing as we both know. In order for you to get there on time we need to leave here early."

He nodded. "I'll drive us back to Ravello and send for the helicopter to take me and Ric to Positano. You must realize this wasn't the way I expected our overnight to go."

She squeezed his hands tighter. "If you want to know the truth, I'm glad she phoned. You need to do this, the sooner the better. Not only for our sake, but for Ric's. Tatania has lost time bonding with him. Of course it's not too late, but I believe Violeta is right. Shock might be the one method to wake her up."

Valentina heard a sharp intake of breath before he lay down on the bed and pulled her into his arms. "What would I do without you?"

"I'm not planning on your finding out," she whispered against his cheek.

"Will you let me hold you tonight?"

"After we held each other on the cruiser, do you have to ask?"

"Yes. What other woman in the world has your ability to love and be so decent at a critical time like this? I want to deserve you."

"Oh, Giovanni." She nestled closer against him.

"You and Vito will be at the house waiting for me when I get back? No more letting anyone else influence you to leave early?"

She burrowed against him. "No one has the power to wrench me from your side." For the rest of the night she held this incredible man in her arms.

At six in the morning after feeding the babies, they left Laurito for Ravello. Giovanni was deep in thought. Paolo and Stanzie were there to greet them when they walked across the patio to the sunroom.

Giovanni hugged them before going upstairs to get ready. Valentina put the babies on the floor and kissed their tummies until their laughter filled the room. While she played with them, she heard the helicopter. He came back to the sunroom. After kissing the boys, he kissed her fiercely.

"I'll be here when you get back," she spoke

before he could say it. Their eyes clung before he put Ric in his carry-cot and wheeled away with him.

Stanzie came in after he'd gone. Her eyes looked anxious. "Is everything all right?"

Valentina sat back on her heels. "It will be, no matter what happens." In the next breath she told Stanzie where he was going and why.

The other woman sank down in a chair. "I wish he would have done this a long time ago. This is *your* doing."

"Don't give me any credit. He wanted to meet with her, but was waiting until Violeta was on board."

"It's a good woman who puts her child's happiness first."

"I couldn't agree more. Please thank Paolo for getting Giovanni back here so fast. His method worked. Except something tells me *you* were the one who came up with the idea."

Stanzie smiled without saying anything.

The day wore on. First lunch, then dinner. By bedtime Valentina realized something important was going on, otherwise he would have been home hours ago. Not until she climbed into bed did she hear the sound on her phone. He'd sent her a text.

Will be home tomorrow. Kiss Vito for me.

Valentina suffered another sleepless night, tossing, turning and worrying. The next morning she looked out the window and discovered a cloudy sky overhead. Hoping it wasn't a bad omen, she went to the nursery to take care of Vito.

By afternoon Giovanni still hadn't arrived. Unable to stand it any longer, she put the baby in the stroller and took a long walk beyond the villa to work off her nervous energy. He slept on and off.

Maybe Giovanni had been in talks with his father about his future with the company. Many thoughts ran through her mind until she was a nervous wreck. Near five o'clock she started back to the villa beneath a darkening sky. On the way, she heard the sound of rotors in the distance. Her heart jumped to look up and see the helicopter overhead.

Giovanni—

She started running as she pushed the stroller along the road. Valentina had walked farther than she'd realized and couldn't believe how long it was taking her to get back. As she turned onto his private road leading up to the side of the villa, she saw Giovanni running toward her. If there weren't good news, he wouldn't be flying down the road to reach her.

The second she could see his eyes, she parked the stroller and ran toward him. He swung her off her feet and clutched her to him without realizing his strength. One look at his face and she saw a different man.

"Violeta's plan worked!"

"I can see that," she answered breathlessly. "Where's Ric?"

"With his mother. She's going to keep him for a few days."

Those words told her everything she needed to know. The guilt he'd been suffering for so long was gone. In its place was a man at peace. "Oh, Giovanni. I'm so happy for you."

"You have no idea."

Yes, she did.

"Violeta drove us to their villa. We talked all day and all night discussing everything, including how to handle visitation. Tatania was like a different person. When she looked at Ric for the first time, I saw a light enter her eyes. It was as if she'd come alive."

"So have you." She cupped the side of his hard jaw with her hand.

He kissed it. "Come on. Let's take Vito and spend the night on the cruiser. I need to tell you everything."

CHAPTER NINE

THE FIRST RAIN of the season hit after Giovanni anchored off Furore, the little mountain village between Ravello and Positano. He'd wanted to show Valentina the fjord where a cluster of old fishermen's houses clung to the side of the rocky gorge. But she wasn't disappointed when the weather forced them to stay below with Vito until the storm passed over. She loved the cozy feeling of having the man and son she loved so close to her.

After eating dinner in the galley, they moved into one of the cabins and put the baby in his carry-cot in the other cabin. She sat on the side of the bed. Giovanni grabbed a pillow and stretched out on the floor.

"I'd come up there with you, but if I do that, I won't be able to talk and we have a lot to discuss. What do you want to know first?"

At last she was going to have answers. "Was Tatania's father there?"

"He walked in the villa after flying in and discovered the four of us in the living room. Ric was cuddled in her arms. Before I could say anything, Tatania told her father that she and I had said our goodbyes, but she'd decided to be a mother to her son. I didn't know she had it in her to stand up to him. Naturally he was nonplussed and walked over to look at the baby."

"That must have been an amazing moment."

"Oh, it was. Tatania had changed before our very eyes. We're going to set up times during the week and every other weekend to parent him. I told her I needed to discuss the schedule with you, then I'd get back to her."

She frowned. "Me—"

"We're partners, Valentina. Everything I do, I plan to run through you first."

Partners? That word again. *Don't panic yet, Valentina.* "Did her father talk to you about your decision to step down?"

"No. His pride won't allow it, but I had a long conversation with my father earlier today. He's aware I want to run the marketing division and is probing the members of the board to see where they would stand."

"That's a beginning."

"Yes. These things take time."

"How did Ric behave with her?"

"As I expected, he started to cry, but then Violeta was there and talked to him. Soon Tatania broke in. The sweetness in her voice touched my heart and soon touched Ric's. He stopped crying and let her feed him a bottle."

Giovanni leaned forward and put his hands on either side of her legs. "It's going to be all right. Thanks to you, Ric is going to grow up with his birth mother, who loves him. If you could have seen her with him… The baby has changed her."

She nodded. "They've changed all of us. That's what babies do."

He was working up to something. "Valentina Montanari, I'm so deeply in love with you, I can't wait any longer for this. While I'm on my knees, will you tell me the thing I want most to hear in this world?"

"That I want to be your wife? As if you didn't know." Suddenly she got down on the floor and showed Giovanni how she felt about him with a kiss that sent him reeling. He rolled her over so he could look down at the beautiful vision before him.

"Right now I could eat you alive and want

to get married right away. Saturday if we can work it."

"Saturday?" she half gasped. "Don't you think we need to give Tatania time to deal with the fact that I'm going to be Ric's step-mother? She's not going to like sharing your baby with me."

"Valentina—she knows we've been living together. Violeta has learned to like you very much. She's seen the loving care you've given Ric. Trust me, it's not going to be a problem."

A shadow crossed over her face. "There are other considerations."

"Name one."

"Maybe we shouldn't get married this fast."

"Why not?"

She searched his eyes. "You haven't even been divorced a year."

"It doesn't matter. No man knows our history except you and me. You know the truth of everything. That's all that's important. We fell madly in love that first day. I need you with me mentally, emotionally and physically as soon as possible."

"I want that, too. You know I do."

"If any couple ever needed a honeymoon, we do." He kissed her again, long and hard.

When next she came up for air she said,

"Don't you know how much I want that, too? But I haven't been for my six-week checkup yet. My doctor warned me to refrain from intimacy until he examines me."

"How soon is your appointment?"

"Next Monday."

"I guess I can wait that long. I want your doctor's seal of approval, too. After we leave his office, we'll get married."

"But how can we do it so fast? Don't we have to wait the customary three weeks?"

"I have connections that solve the problem. But I'm being selfish. If you want a big wedding that takes weeks and maybe months to plan, we'll do it."

She shook her head. "I think we're both way beyond that."

"Grazie a Dio."

A soft laugh escaped her lips he couldn't stop tasting.

"Where do you want to be married, *adorata*?" After he'd asked the question, he kissed her mouth again and again. She'd become his addiction. When she didn't answer right away he said, "I'm going too fast for you, aren't I?"

"No." She pressed her forehead against his. "It's what I love about you. No grass grows under your feet. Is there a church that has special meaning for you?"

"This wedding isn't about me."

"There's a church in Naples near my parents' villa the family has attended, but I don't have a favorite place. Something tells me you do."

"If the truth be known, I like the countryside church outside Laurito."

"The little white one hidden in the trees?"

"You remember?" He kissed her neck.

"Of course. I found it charming."

"For years I've been friends with the older priest who presides there."

She smiled at him. "Somehow that doesn't surprise me. Your ancestors came from that area."

"What would you think if he marries us in a private ceremony? Afterward we'll stay at the quaint *locanda* nearby for the night and drive home to the children the next day. Maybe two weeks after that we'll throw a party at the villa for our families to announce our marriage. When we're sure the babies can handle it, we'll take an extended honeymoon."

She wound her arms around his neck. "You know exactly what I think. I'm fathoms deep in love with you, Giovanni. My heart and soul are yours, but you've been aware of that from the first. It's embarrassing how transparent I've been."

"Embarrassing?"

"That first night when we took the babies home, I couldn't wait for morning. If you hadn't phoned, I would have phoned you. I thought to myself, 'Signor Laurito will make this all right.' Even then, I knew you had the answers for my whole life."

"I had a revelation that you were the answer to mine," he said in a half-savage tone. "Do you have any idea how long I've been waiting to hear those words?"

He reached in his pocket and pulled out a blue diamond ring mounted in white gold. Finding her left hand, he found her ring finger and slid it home. "I had this made for you two weeks ago, but needed to find the right time to give it to you."

Valentina held it up. "It's beautiful. Oh, my love—" She pressed a hot kiss to his mouth. "*You're* such a beautiful man, I can't stop looking at you."

Giovanni chuckled. "Don't let anyone else hear you say that."

"Any woman who hears me will be thinking the same thing."

He plundered her mouth once more. "We've got things to do. If you want to go to school, you know I'm behind you on that. Whatever happens we're going to do everything together. You'll have to cancel on your apartment."

"I can't think about anything right now. You've just proposed and I'm the happiest woman who ever lived."

She didn't know the half of it. "Do you think your father is still awake? I'd like to phone him and tell him how much I love his angelic daughter."

"He has trouble sleeping. I'm sure a phone call from you will bring him a lot of peace. He's been worried about me. While you do that, I'll phone Rini. I want him to know our plans. He won't say anything."

"Let's do it in a minute. I need another kiss to let me know I'm not dreaming all this."

"Papà?" It was Sunday night. Giovanni had been waiting at the villa for the important call from him. Valentina was downstairs playing with the babies on the patio. "What's the verdict?"

"Not good, *figlio mio*."

"That means Salvatore has garnered enough votes to keep me out."

"Afraid so. He's outraged that you're living with Valentina."

"So being a grandfather hasn't softened him up. For Tatania's sake, that's too bad."

"My concern is for you. What are you going to do?"

"I have something in mind I've been considering for months."

"What is that?"

"I'm going to branch out on my own, but it's a subject for another day. I'll be in touch with you again soon. Give Mamma my love."

"Giovanni—wait!"

"I have to go. *Buonanotte*, Papà."

He left the bedroom and went downstairs to the kitchen. Stanzie and Paolo were eating dinner. "I'm glad you're both here. We need to talk." He sat down at the table with them.

Stanzie's eyes lit up. "Is this what I think? I saw the diamond on her finger. It's the same blue as her eyes."

Giovanni was warmed by her excitement. "The closest match I could find. After her doctor appointment tomorrow, we'll be getting married at the church in Laurito in an evening ceremony."

A gasp of excitement came from Stanzie.

"We don't want to wait. Except for her father and brother, no one else knows but you. I've made all the arrangements. It'll be a totally private ceremony with my old friend Father Mancini officiating.

"Would you two mind tending the *bambini* overnight tomorrow night? We'll be staying at the inn near the church and come home on Tuesday. We don't plan to take a long honeymoon for several months."

"Of course we'll watch over them. We love them!" she cried.

"Thank you, Stanzie. After we get back I plan to talk business with the two of you."

Paolo stopped chewing. "What do you mean?"

"I'm not working for the family business anymore. That association has come to an end. With hindsight I can see it's a good thing to get away from all the nepotism that ties hands. A while back I purchased office space in Naples as an investment for the future. I'm glad I did because I plan to start my own advertising agency. I'd hoped your uncle would sell his business to me so you could run it, but that hope has died."

"You would have done that for us?" Paolo looked incredulous.

"Of course, but no matter. My attorney is drawing up the paperwork now for a new business. I'm calling it PSG Advertising. The letters stand for Paolo, Stanzie and yours truly. You'll be part owners with me in charge of putting all your great innovative ideas to work while I drum up business and bring in new accounts. I already have half a dozen possible clients in mind who have no association with my family's business."

The two of them sat there speechless while their eyes misted over.

"Though we'll keep your apartment here at the villa for you whenever you come to visit, I'm aware you'd love to get back to your house in Naples. All our lives have been on hold for too long.

"I want to be a full-time father and husband. Owning a business like this will require hard work, but it won't force me to give up my soul. My personal life is the most important thing to me.

"Valentina will go back to school for her degree. After she graduates, she'll find work as an engineer, but she'll make sure it doesn't interfere with being a wife and helping me raise our boys."

"Who will help you here?"

"We'll find someone from the village to come in periodically, but Valentina insists she wants to be in charge of the house. She and I are a team."

"We are," Valentina piped up. She'd entered the kitchen. Giovanni had no idea how long she'd been listening. She walked over and put her arms around his neck from behind. "You two should know you're the role model for us. Last night we talked about how amazing you are. A husband and wife who love to be together and love what they do is a rare phenomenon."

Giovanni kissed her arm. "They've agreed to watch the children until we get back on Tuesday."

"Congratulations on your coming marriage," Paolo murmured. "When Giovanni first brought you here, Stanzie and I agreed you were the angel who'd come to bless his life."

"It's the other way around. He's my prince. No woman in the world is as lucky as I am. The baby switch threw us into the darkest abyss. Only a loving man and father was able to perform the miracle that brought us into the light."

"Ready, Valentina?"

"Almost." The next time Giovanni caught sight of her, he'd see a woman who burned to become his bride.

She put on the knee-length ivory wedding dress. The color matched her strappy high heels. The slim-form chiffon swished around her legs. Three-quarter-length sleeves and the modest V-neck bodice of illusion lace gave it an ethereal look.

After giving her hair a quick brushing, she applied softshell-pink lipstick to her lips. When she'd gone shopping for a dress, she'd found some gold earrings with blue jewels. The last thing she did was pin on the corsage of creamy roses he'd left in her room.

"Hurry," he called to her.

With heart pounding she walked out in the hall and started for the staircase. The second he saw her coming down, he took several pictures with his phone before putting it back in his pocket.

Her husband-to-be looked magnificent in an expensive light gray suit. Against the white of his shirt he wore a striped silver-and-gray tie. His black eyes smoldered as she walked up to him. "I didn't know anyone so beautiful could be real," he whispered in an unsteady voice. Heat filled her cheeks.

He was so gorgeous she ached inside for him. "I can't wait to be married to you."

Giovanni sucked in his breath. "I can tell you just put on lipstick, but I have to kiss you." She was already there, leaning toward him. With a fierce hunger, she welcomed his compelling mouth.

Both of them moaned with need before he helped her into the helicopter. The heavenly scent filled the interior. For the rest of the short trip to Laurito she floated on a cloud of euphoria. He gripped her hand. "Did you say goodbye to the children?"

"I didn't dare."

He kissed her palm. "Neither did I. We have to hope they behave."

A limo was waiting for them when they reached Laurito. Giovanni directed the driver to the church and instructed him to wait until they came back out.

"Ready?" he whispered, hugging her to his side.

Breathing in the marvelous scent of him,

she kissed his smooth, shaven cheek before they entered the doors. No one was inside except the priest and two church workers there to witness the marriage. They walked down the aisle to the altar. The interior of the small church with its frescoes of the saints lent a spiritual essence she would always remember.

"Father Mancini?" Giovanni shook his hand and introduced Valentina.

The older priest smiled at her. "I have known Giovanni Laurito for a long time. You have made him very happy, Signorina Montanari. He says he's in a great hurry to marry you."

"We're both impatient, Father."

"Then we won't waste any more time. Giovanni? Take Valentina by the hand and repeat after me."

Thus began the sacred ceremony. When Giovanni pledged his love and devotion to her, the words wound straight to her heart. She professed her love and devotion to him with the same solemnity. "I now pronounce you man and wife, in the name of the Father, the Son and the Holy Spirit. Amen."

He made the sign of the cross. "Do you have rings to exchange?"

"We do," Giovanni spoke up and slid the matching gold band next to her blue diamond.

Valentina took the gold ring she'd bought him from off the finger of her right hand and slid it onto the ring finger of his left hand.

The priest nodded. "You may now kiss your bride."

"At last," Giovanni murmured before his mouth descended on hers. The first kiss from her husband thrilled her so much her legs buckled. He had to prop her up.

Father Mancini cleared his voice, reminding her they had an audience. Again she blushed before Giovanni finally let her go. "I'll follow you to the vestibule where you'll sign your name to the marriage document."

Giovanni put her arm through his and they made the trip to the entrance. Normally the church would have been overflowing with guests. Their ceremony was private, unique, and she loved every moment of it.

The priest stood by while they signed their names. Then he added his signature and dated it before rolling it up and handing it to her. "Come and worship often."

"We will, Father," Valentina assured him.

"I'm adopting her son, Vitielli. As soon as

it becomes legal, we'll be coming to you to baptize him."

"Ah. And what about your son, Giovanni?"

"His mother will make the arrangements with her priest in Positano."

"Excellent."

Valentina shook his hand. "Thank you, Father."

Giovanni put his arm around her waist and ushered her out of the church to the limo. He gave the chauffeur directions to the inn where they were staying. She was relieved the drive only took about two minutes. Valentina couldn't wait to be alone with him.

They carried their overnight bags into the reception area of the charming getaway tucked in the greenery. After obtaining the key, Giovanna cupped her arm and they walked down the hall to their room. The place was a restored farmhouse, completely enchanting. When the door shut, enclosing them, she felt that they'd entered a world from another century.

"Come here, Signora Laurito. You don't know how long I've been waiting to say that." She moved toward him. He unpinned the flowers from her dress and put them on the dresser. "There's something we haven't done yet. It's time I found out what it's like to dance with my wife. I want to feel every part of you."

He drew her into his arms. For a little while they moved in place. He kissed her neck, her ears and throat. When his lips brushed across her cheeks and temples, she couldn't stop trembling. All the time he was driving her crazy as he kissed her everywhere except her mouth, he was undoing the buttons on the back of her dress.

Her hands slid up the shirt covering his well-defined chest to undo his tie. "Kiss me, *caro*."

Their wedding night began with a giving and taking that took Valentina to a place she'd never known existed. She couldn't recall how one minute they were standing, and the next he'd taken her to bed. From the moment he touched her, desire licked through her body like flames that grew hotter and more intense.

"I love you, Giovanni. No one should love someone the way I love you."

"I love the things you say to me and the way you say them. Give me your mouth again, *innamorata*. I can't live without it."

Throughout the rest of the night they loved with abandon. The pleasure they gave each other was exquisite beyond belief. This was her husband thrilling her. She felt sorry for every woman who would never know what it was like to be loved by him.

"Don't ever stop loving me, Valentina," he begged. "Don't ever let me go or I'd die in agony."

"Giovanni, darling—just try to get away from me and you'll see what happens. You've done something to me. I'm on fire for you. Love me again."

"I intend to. Over and over."

When morning came she awakened first, shocked to see how late it was. Her gorgeous husband lay on his side with his arm around her hip. Even in sleep he was possessive of her in a way that touched her heart.

For a while she studied his face, the way his black lashes fanned against his olive skin. The black hair she'd disheveled gave him a dashing look. He needed a shave. She rubbed her cheek against his jaw to be closer to him.

He must have felt her because his eyes opened. His black gaze enveloped her before he pulled her on top of him. "I was dreaming about you."

One corner of her mouth lifted. "While you were watching you, I was watching you. Do you realize something amazing happened last night?"

"After what went on for hours and hours, what kind of a question is that?" Giovanni kissed a favorite spot.

"We didn't eat dinner. I've never known you not to be hungry before."

"You've cast a spell over me." His eyes burned like dark fires. "I have a different kind of hunger." He started loving her again until she felt immortal. When next she came awake, she found her husband looking at her.

"You're incredibly beautiful, do you know that?"

"I hope you'll always be able to say that to me. I love you, Giovanni. I'm so happy to be your wife I can hardly believe we're married. I loved our wedding."

"It was perfect."

"I don't want any of this to end. How soon do we have to leave here?"

"How about never."

"I hope the babies are behaving."

"Do you miss them?"

"I'll be honest and tell you I didn't think about them until just now." She heard a knock on the door. "Who do you suppose that is?"

"I ordered breakfast." He reached for his

robe and put it on to answer the door. In a few minutes he brought the tray to their bed and they ate with relish.

"Valentina? There's one subject we haven't talked about."

"What's that?"

"Actually it's all we've talked about since we met, but not in the context I'm thinking of now."

"You mean about us having our own baby?"

He nodded. "You read me like a book."

"It's been on my mind, too. Yesterday Dr. Pedrotti said he hoped he wouldn't need to see me unless I was pregnant again."

"Do you think it's possible that one day you'll want to have our baby?"

Valentina moved the tray to the floor before pushing him back against the pillows. "It hurts that you would ask that question in such a defeated tone of voice. You might as well have asked me if I thought the world was going to end tomorrow.

"Of course I want a baby with you! I know you missed out on the thrill of going through Tatania's pregnancy with her. I missed out on having a husband around while I was carrying Vito."

"But I know you want to work as an engineer one day. For you to have another baby requires a lot of sacrifice."

"Darling—I want a baby with you more than anything in the world. I was hoping we could try for one when the boys start to walk."

His eyes lit up. "You mean it? You're not just saying it to humor me?"

She kissed him for a long time. "Wouldn't it be fantastic to have a girl?"

"Fantastic," he murmured. "She'll have golden locks."

"Whatever you say, Giovanni. I know you think bigger and faster than anyone else. But for now let's concentrate on us. The only thing I want to do is make love to my husband. I've been dreaming about it for weeks."

"So have I." His smile looked wicked. "I'm waiting."

CHAPTER TEN

Two weeks later

AS VALENTINA STEPPED out of the shower and wrapped a towel around herself, Giovanni walked inside the bathroom. His eyes blazed like hot black fires, scorching her everywhere he looked. "With guests arriving in the next half hour, you shouldn't be this ravishing or I'll have a heart attack and there'll be no groom for our families to congratulate on our recent wedding."

She flashed him a mysterious smile. "Should I have locked the door?"

He caught her in his arms. "It wouldn't do any good. I'd knock it down to get to you." So saying, he kissed her mouth until she felt faint with longing. When he lifted his head, he said, "I can tell you're trembling. Something tells me you're a little nervous."

Valentina lifted anxious eyes to him. "I just want everything to go all right."

Giovanni kissed the end of her well-shaped nose. "As long as you and I are all right, nothing else matters. Besides, we hold the trump card."

"What do you mean?"

"The children."

Her lips relaxed into a smile. "Of course. They look so darling in their little tuxedo outfits I can hardly stand it."

"Why don't we hold our sons so that when everyone arrives, the children will be the first thing they see and any other thoughts they had about our quick marriage will fly out the window."

"That's a perfect idea!" She pressed a kiss to his compelling mouth. "Now I need to get dressed."

"Let me help you."

"Giovanni—"

"You're blushing all over."

"Stop!"

"Ti amo, Signora Laurito."

"Ti amo, Signor Laurito."

Twenty minutes later she and Giovanni had dressed in their wedding clothes and went downstairs to the patio, where Stanzie and Paolo were tending the children in their swings. Valentina's eyes filled with happy tears to see the babies all decked out in little black tuxedo suit coats and ties with white shirts and black pants.

Giovanni had hired a videographer to come and film the entire evening. Classical music played in the background. Flowers from the garden filled the house and the tables set up outside on the terrace. Torches illuminated the pool area and fabulous banquet table overflowing with sumptuous food and champagne. He pinned a corsage of gardenias on her shoulder and kissed her once more.

Paolo gave them the heads-up that people were arriving. On cue, Valentina and Giovanni picked up their boys and stood together to start welcoming their families. Giovanni's family walked out on the patio followed by Valentina's. Rini pushed her father's wheelchair right up to Valentina so she could kiss her father. Bianca had come with them.

The minute everyone saw the babies, there was pandemonium. The younger children rushed over to play with them. Everyone wanted to hold and kiss them. Valentina glanced at her handsome husband. "Your idea was ingenious," she whispered. "Another Giovanni Laurito takeover. No one stood a chance."

His deep happy laughter traveled through her entire body. She loved this man with a passion she couldn't begin to express.

With all the attention, their babies clung to them. He grasped Valentina's hand and cleared his throat. "Welcome, everyone. Valentina and I are thrilled you could come to celebrate our marriage. We were married two weeks ago at the church in Laurito and are ecstatically happy.

"Our babies refused to be comforted unless we were both with them. You might say they were responsible for this marriage that has been founded on nothing but love from the first moment Valentina and I laid eyes on each other.

"Please enjoy yourselves for the rest of the night, but we have no idea how long our boys will last with all this excitement."

Valentina and Giovanni met each other's families and rejoiced that Vito and Ric would have so many little cousins to grow up with. Maybe twenty minutes into the evening, two more people arrived. Valentina sucked in her breath.

It was Violeta and...Tatania, Ric's beautiful, black-haired mother.

"I'm glad they came," Giovanni murmured, "but I'm not surprised Salvatore isn't with them. Excuse me for a minute."

She watched Giovanni carry Ric over to her and place him in her arms. Ric had spent enough time with his mother that he didn't fuss at being passed to her. Giovanni came back and slid his arm around Valentina's waist.

"*Grazie a Dio* you convinced me to talk to her. Tell me the truth. Does it hurt to see him respond to her?"

Valentina stared up at him with tear-filled eyes. "Not at all. She's *his* mother. I have my son, Vito, and the memories of Ric being mine for those first two and a half weeks. No one can take that away from me. And of course, I have you. What more could I want in this entire world?"

"*Bellissima*—I can't wait to get you alone tonight."

"I'm way ahead of you and have already started the countdown."

His burst of laughter caused heads to turn

in their direction. Valentina's wonderful husband sounded so happy, she shared a smile
with Stanzie and Paolo, who knew the pain
he'd been through and were overjoyed for
him.

* * * * *

*Look out for THE BILLIONAIRE WHO
SAW HER BEAUTY, the second book in the*
MONTANARI MARRIAGES *duet*

COMING NEXT MONTH FROM

⊞ HARLEQUIN®
™

Romance

Available May 10, 2016

#4519 THE BILLIONAIRE WHO SAW HER BEAUTY
The Montanari Marriages
by Rebecca Winters

Shy socialite Alessandra Caracciolo doesn't believe she'll find love after being betrayed. Yet Alessandra feels an instant connection with billionaire Rinieri Montanari. He's the first man to have eyes only for her... but can she be brave enough to believe in their love?

#4520 IN THE BOSS'S CASTLE
The Life Swap
by Jessica Gilmore

Maddison Carter's job swap is the start of a new life—until she's tempted by off-limits boss Kit Buchanan! When she's whisked to his Scottish castle, Maddison realizes that with Kit by her side she doesn't need the perfect past to have the perfect future...

#4521 ONE WEEK WITH THE FRENCH TYCOON
by Christy McKellen

Indigo Hughes books a holiday for one on the Amalfi Coast, but instead of peace and quiet, she's thrown together with cynical, sexy tycoon Julien Moreaux. He's the type of man she should avoid, but big-hearted Indigo hopes to help Julien find his faith in love again.

#4522 RAFAEL'S CONTRACT BRIDE
by Nina Milne

Rafael Martinez needs Cora Brooks's hand in marriage to close a crucial business deal. Cora knows his unexpected proposal is only for a paper marriage, but as Rafael helps her step out of the shadows she hopes their wedding vows might last a lifetime!

———————

YOU CAN FIND MORE INFORMATION ON UPCOMING HARLEQUIN® TITLES, FREE EXCERPTS AND MORE AT WWW.HARLEQUIN.COM.

HRLPCNM0416

LARGER-PRINT BOOKS!

GET 2 FREE LARGER-PRINT NOVELS PLUS

2 FREE GIFTS!

HARLEQUIN®

Romance

From the Heart, For the Heart

*Maddison Carter's job swap is the start of a new life—
until she's tempted by off-limits boss Kit Buchanan and
whisked to his Scottish castle!*

*Read on for a sneak preview of
IN THE BOSS'S CASTLE, the first
in Jessica Gilmore's heartwarming duet
THE LIFE SWAP*

"It's not a race, Maddison. Slow down and smell the roses—or at least enjoy the view."

"Slowing down is for losers. You'd be eaten alive in Manhattan," she threw back. "No! Darn it! Ugh. I'm trapped in a swamp! Kit! Stop laughing…"

He came up beside her, slow and easy, folding his arms and eyes dancing with amusement as he took her in. "Pride comes before a fall."

"I haven't fallen." Maddison tried to summon some shred of dignity, hard as it was to do when one foot was caught fast in a mini swamp, the other scrabbling for a firm foothold. Any minute now she was going to tumble and she'd be damned if she was going to fall in front of this man. Any man.

"Yet," Kit pointed out helpfully.

"You could help me."

"I could." The laughter underpinned his words and she glared at him.

"Do you want me to beg?"

"Well…" He leaned in close and her breath hitched.

His face was barely centimeters from he
close enough to grab, to hold on to, to bu
let herself be saved.

She didn't need saving, did she? Just a he

"You could say *please*."

Their eyes caught, held. His were alive with laughter,
a teasing warmth curving his mouth, but behind the
amusement was something hotter, something deeper,
something straining to break through. And Maddison knew,
with utter certainty, that all she needed to do was ask.

She glared, watching his amusement increase until a
reluctant smile curved her lips. "Please."

"There, that wasn't so hard, was it?" Kit grasped her
hand and pulled. "Easy, Maddison, I got you."

He had. His arms were around her, steadying her,
holding her up, and she allowed herself to be held, to be
steadied. Just for a second. What harm could it do? One
moment of needing someone else? Just a moment and
then she would pull back, make some quip and carry on,
because that was what Maddison Carter did, right? She
carried on.

"Thanks." Her breath was short, and as she looked into
his eyes, any urge to laugh the moment off fell away. All the
amusement had drained out of his face, out of those blue
eyes, now impossibly molten like sapphire forged in some
great furnace. Instead she looked into the sharp planes of his
face and saw want. She saw need. She saw desire.

For her.